KIKI
AND
JACQUES

KIKI
AND
JACQUES

Susan Ross

Holiday House / New York

HOLIDAY HOUSE is registered in the U.S. Patent and Trademark Office.
Printed and bound in November 2018 at Maple Press, York, PA, USA.
3 5 7 9 10 8 6 2
www.holidayhouse.com
Library of Congress Cataloging-in-Publication Data

Ross, Susan L.
Kiki and Jacques / Susan Ross.
— First edition.
pages cm
Summary: "Eleven-year-old Jacques, who must contend with difficult family
dynamics and pressure from an older boy to help him commit a crime, is surprised to
discover that he has much in common with Kiki, one of the many new Somali refugees
who have immigrated to his Maine town"— Provided by publisher.
ISBN 978-0-8234-3427-5 (hardcover)
[1. Friendship—Fiction. 2. Somali Americans—Fiction. 3. Refugees—Fiction.
4. Prejudices—Fiction. 5. Maine—Fiction.] I. Title.
PZ7.1.R73Ki 2015
[Fic]—dc23
2014038413

ISBN 978-0-8234-4180-8 (paperback)

*To William, Erik, and Sarah—
filling our lives with love,
laughter, and stories.*

1

"I'm not going out there." Jacques Gagnon shook his head, curls flying, and planted his feet at the dressing room door. "I know that girl!"

Grandmère Jeannette lifted a long white wedding dress from the rack. "I'm sorry, but I can't do this alone . . . grab the train and make sure it don't drag."

Jacques's heart was pounding in his ears. He'd helped out in Grandmère Jeannette's bridal shop ever since he could remember; that was no big deal. But now, Monique St. Hilaire, the coolest senior at Lakemont High, sat with her mother on the old leather couch in the salesroom. Monique and Jacques both went to church at St. Francis; nearly every boy in his confirmation class had a crush on her. Her straight blonde hair was divided with a red streak, and she was quietly chewing on purple colored nails.

Grandmère Jeannette straightened her glasses and stormed ahead. "I have a real special wedding gown for you."

"Yeah, whatever." Monique glanced up without smiling.

"This one's super hot!" Jacques gagged on his tongue. He swallowed hard and held his breath, waiting for Monique to say how stupid he sounded.

But Monique simply crossed her long legs and turned away. She didn't seem to notice him at all.

Jacques's face was steaming as he bolted up the narrow steps to the office loft above the sales floor. He could hear Monique moan, "Let's get out of here," before the shop door slammed shut. Hoisting himself onto the old oak desk, Jacques thwacked the wood with his heels and gazed through the windows to the street, his heart still thumping with humiliation.

"Grandmère—look!" Two black women dressed in long skirts and flowing shawls were leaning against the display window, peering in.

"What is it, *mon cher*?"

"Some African ladies. They have scarves around their heads." Over the past few years, refugees from Africa had come to southern Maine, but for the first time, at the beginning of the summer, a group of Somali families had moved to Lakemont.

"Are you sure? You suppose they want to buy something?" Grandmère Jeannette went to the window as Jacques scrambled down the stairs, but the women were gone.

The front door jingled, and Sammy Baker stepped inside, a soccer ball under his arm. Sammy was short, with brown hair and a mouth full of braces. The boys had been best friends since kindergarten, maybe even preschool.

"Hey dude, you ready to go?"

"I still have some stuff to put away."

Sammy rolled his eyes. "Soccer tryouts are next week, and you're busy sorting dresses?"

Jacques shrugged and took one hopeful step toward the door.

"Scoot before I change my mind." Grandmère Jeannette smiled as usual with her pink lips shut. Jacques knew she was shy about showing off the large gap between her teeth. "Be home early. I might've baked a pie for dinner, seeing how it's your birthday tomorrow. Father Lazar asked me to run the Bingo game at church tomorrow night, so we'll celebrate this evening."

Jacques grinned, and Sammy licked the edge of his mouth.

"You come too, Sammy—I'll phone your folks." Grandmère Jeannette winked and tapped Jacques's backside with a rolled magazine as the boys ducked out the door.

They started down Main Street, past the Army Navy Store and Yvonne's House of Pizza. The cracked sidewalks were lined with small shops, some with signs in the window, *Ici On Parle Français*, but there were hardly any shoppers.

Across the road from the Army Navy Store, a teenage boy in a dark hoodie stood beside a fire hydrant, smoking. He had thick black hair and a thin line under his nose. When he spotted Jacques, he tossed the cigarette in the gutter and side-kicked the hydrant for no reason.

"Let's head the other way. It's quicker," Jacques said.

"No, it's not." Sammy looked puzzled; then he noticed the older boy. "Isn't that Duane? I thought he was in jail or something."

"I wish," Jacques muttered.

Duane lived in the neighborhood and went to church at St. Francis, but he was mean and unpredictable. Most kids kept clear of him. Duane had dropped out of high school last winter, a few months before graduation. The rumor was he'd been arrested for stealing cars; no one had seen him all summer.

Duane raised one arm and shouted, "Hey Gagnon, get over here!"

"Stay away from us." Jacques darted across the street with Sammy trailing after him.

"What was that about?" Sammy asked.

Jacques shook his head. "I've got no idea." Jacques was afraid to tell anyone—even Sammy—that Duane had stopped him in front of the library a week ago and asked him to sell pot at school. Jacques had refused and run away.

Jacques stopped and grabbed Sammy's arm. "Look over there!"

The two Somali women stood a few feet away. The shorter lady lifted her head, and Jacques realized that she wasn't a woman at all, but a girl about his age. The girl met his gaze for a second, and he thought he saw her smile. She had smooth brown skin and large dark

4

eyes. Her hair, neck and shoulders were completely covered by a wide blue scarf.

Sammy nudged Jacques. "We better go."

"Wait a minute." Jacques took another look. Beside her left eye, a long jagged scar shimmered down the side of the girl's face. The older Somali lady caught him staring. She swung her arm and pulled the girl away. It sounded like she was scolding, though Jacques couldn't make out any of the words.

"Did you see the scar?" Sammy asked.

"What'd you think happened to her?" Jacques paused, balancing the soccer ball on one knee.

"I dunno. . . . Something bad." Sammy tilted his head. "She's kinda cute, though."

"I didn't notice." Jacques grinned.

"Yeah, right." Sammy grinned back.

2

As the boys approached the soccer field, Jacques could see a huddle in the distance. Coach Morrin was off to one side, checking his clipboard.

"Listen, don't mention the thing at the shop to anyone, okay?"

"You mean the fact that you sell wedding dresses to hottie high school girls?"

Jacques knocked his shoulder into Sammy's back, but Sammy simply laughed. "What's the matter, maybe you like Monique a little?"

"It's just weird that she's getting married! I wonder who the dude is?" Jacques frowned. "Doesn't Monique want to go to college?"

Frank Boucher broke out from the pack and dribbled the ball toward the goal; in a minute he sliced it in. Boucher was tall, and broader than most of the kids. His bleach-blond hair was spiked marine-style, making him look even larger.

"Holy crap." Jacques whistled. "That wasn't bad."

"You'll be captain," Sammy said. "Don't worry. Boucher's got muscle but your footwork's better. And nobody trusts him."

"Wait up—who's that kid?" Jacques nodded toward the far end of the field. "That big dude . . . is he one of the Somalis?"

A slim black teenager was dribbling toward them. Fast and accurate, the ball skipped effortlessly from side to side. The boy balanced the ball between his shin and knees, spun around and took a wild shot from midfield. Tim O'Shea knocked his glasses off trying to stop it, but the ball slipped right past him into the goal.

"What the . . . !" Jacques exclaimed.

"Whoa." Sammy clasped his face in his hands. "That was insane."

"Hey Gagnon!" Boucher jogged over. "You seen the Somali dude yet?"

"Yeah, we see him alright."

"Moved here last month. My dad says a lot more Africans are coming to Maine. He says Somali kids are gonna be at school this year."

"You're kidding," Sammy said.

"The dude can kick, but he barely speaks English." Boucher spit on the ground.

"That kid's got a heck of a foot. He just hit the goal from thirty yards." Jacques spit too.

"I guess," Boucher said. "But he won't understand the plays. I doubt Coach will let him on the team."

Out of the corner of his eyes, Jacques could see the new kid driving the ball toward the opposite goal. He was fast, wicked fast.

Suddenly, Boucher ran back on the field. Lunging ahead of the new kid, he slowed and threw his weight into his side. For a moment, the boy lost his balance, and it looked like he might go down, but with a half twist, he pulled the ball away and soared down the field, gone.

Jacques's mouth hung open. "Boucher chucked him his hardest, and he didn't even drop."

Coach Morrin blew the whistle and waved the boys in. Boucher was panting as he held his hands to his ribs, but the new boy was breathing slow and steady.

"I want you all to work hard this year, but help each other out, too." Coach Morrin surveyed the group. "A winning team means teamwork."

Jacques sucked on his cheek, while Boucher yawned loudly. Tim O'Shea took off his goalie gloves and fiddled with his glasses. Coach Morrin taught science at the high school. He was fair and steady, but prone to making lengthy speeches about sportsmanship. The boys had heard this all before. The tryouts were what mattered.

The new kid stood apart, staring straight ahead. He didn't even blink.

"One more item. . . ." Coach Morrin cleared his throat. "We got a fresh recruit here today." Jacques and Sammy glanced at each other. "This is Mohamed—he's just movin' into the area, but judging from what I've seen so far, we can definitely use his skills."

No one said a word. Coach Morrin turned his head toward the new boy, who didn't speak or smile.

Jacques looked carefully at Mohamed. He was tall, even taller than Boucher, and he had muscles bulging beneath his T-shirt that made Jacques feel puny.

"Now get on out there!" Coach Morrin exclaimed. "You guys have exactly a week to show me what you got."

3

"He wasn't that good," Sammy mumbled as they headed home from practice.

"No, he was only amazing." Jacques kicked a stone off the sidewalk.

"You'll still be captain!" Sammy exclaimed. "The new kid can't just show up and take over, and anyway, Boucher's right, he barely said a word."

"He's crazy fast, way faster than me. How much jabbering do you need for that?" Jacques shook his head, thinking what to say when he got home. Dad expected him to be captain.

The boys walked in silence past a row of brick tenement buildings. Laundry hung off the fire escapes, and the parking spaces were littered with hubcaps, broken bicycles and pieces of toys.

Jacques and his father lived with Grandmère Jeannette at the end of the block on the top floor of a shingled two-family house with a small yard. His grandparents had moved into the apartment as soon as they'd gotten married; Grandmère Jeannette kept it after his grandfather died. Dad was an only child, and Jacques's bedroom was the same room his father had grown up in. There was a narrow bed next to a closet and a window set over built-in pine drawers. From Jacques's window you could see the old Lakemont Mill, shuttered and decaying, rising above the neighborhood park with its cracked pavement and creaky swing set.

"There's Duane again." Sammy slowed down.

Duane was alone at the far end of the park, shifting from one foot to the other. His hands were stuffed deep in his pockets.

"I bet he's selling drugs," Sammy whispered.

Jacques grunted, his stomach starting to churn. "C'mon, we're already late."

Duane pulled out one hand, and for a split second, a glint of steel flashed before disappearing back into his hoodie.

"Was that a knife?" Sammy exclaimed.

"Let's go." Jacques gulped and pushed Sammy, up the stairs to the apartment.

As they walked in the door, he spotted a pile of gifts on the floor. Jacques wanted a soccer jersey for his birthday, and he wanted it bad. His favorite team was Arsenal, and everybody knew it.

"Hey, the birthday boy's home." Dad lay sprawled on the living room couch watching TV, a beer can in one hand. Donny Gagnon had heavy arms and a wide neck, and his stomach peeked out from the bottom of his shirt.

"Hi, Dad." A white rabbit with a brown nose hopped into the room. "Pelé!" Jacques scooped the rabbit into his arms, and Sammy scratched behind its ears. Jacques had named Pelé after his favorite soccer player, the greatest striker of all time.

"Watch out that bunny don't poop on the couch." Grandmère Jeannette appeared from the kitchen. "*Mon père*, may he rest in peace, he liked a good *lapin* stew."

Jacques shot Sammy a "she's insane" look, but smiled as he rubbed Pelé's back. Grandmère Jeannette loved the rabbit nearly as much as he did. She was always feeding him bits of carrot or apple peels and talking to him about her *lapin*-shooting father from Quebec.

"How was practice?" Dad got another beer from the fridge and handed the boys Cokes as they sat down to dinner. The dining room and living room were barely separated by an open arch, so Jacques could see Pelé hop onto the faded green couch and make himself comfortable—Grandmère Jeannette was obviously pretending not to notice.

Dad took a slug of beer. "You're a shoe-in for captain this year, am I right?"

"There's a new Somali kid," Jacques said. "He's good."

"No kiddin'." Dad scratched the stubble under his chin.

"Not just good," Sammy added. "The dude is awesome."

"Huh," Dad grunted.

"Jacques saw some Somali ladies outside the shop today." Grandmère Jeannette set a platter of fried chicken wings and drumsticks on the table. "Strange, Africans moving up here when everybody knows that Lakemont's mostly French Canadian."

"Grandmère," Jacques interrupted, "Sammy's family isn't Canadian." Sammy was Jewish, and his parents were from Cleveland, not Quebec. But Jacques had to admit that most of his friends had relatives from Canada and went to church at St. Francis, where the late-afternoon Mass was held in French on Sundays.

Grandmère Jeannette's cheeks flared. "I'm real sorry, Sammy!"

Dad picked up a chicken wing and turned to Jacques. "You'll be showing this new kid a thing or two, right?"

Jacques felt a sharp pain hit his stomach. "I dunno, Dad. . . . Like I said, the new guy's talented."

"You're not going to let this kid move in and make captain," Dad replied. "No way."

Jacques looked down at his plate, silent. What was he supposed to do?

"Wait 'til you see my pie." Grandmère Jeannette rose and hustled toward the kitchen. "It's called Triple Threat Chocolate. I got the recipe from Lucy Labelle's aunt." She returned with a pie smothered in fudge and topped with twelve slightly dented red and yellow striped candles. The same candles from Dad's cake last month, Jacques realized.

"That Lucy's a sweet girl, don't you think?" Grandmère Jeannette winked.

"She's okay, I guess." Now Jacques was the one feeling his face go red.

It was finally time to open presents. The first package was soft and squishy, and Jacques glanced at Sammy with a surge of hope. As soon as he pulled off the wrapping, though, he realized how stupid he'd been.

"Thanks for the fleece. My old one was way small."

Dad had found work last spring in the back office of L.L. Bean. Jacques was the most warmly dressed kid at school, but he longed for stuff that wasn't bought with an employee discount. He ripped through the rest of his gifts: two flannel shirts—one that still had a tag that said "returned"—a bag of socks and a gym bag. He sighed and searched beneath the pile of gift wrap, just in case.

"Wicked cool gear" Sammy whispered. Jacques kicked him under the table.

"Somethin' wrong?" Grandmère Jeannette lifted her glasses.

"No, it's just that . . ."

"Money's real tight right now, *mon cher.*"

"That's enough; you don't need to worry the boy." Dad spoke sharply, then turned toward Jacques. "Listen, buddy, I've been thinking about this Somali kid. It's high time you toughen up. If your coach was workin' you hard, like when I was playing ball, you'd be rock solid by now."

"I'm plenty tough, Dad! Kids at school don't mess with me or anything." Jacques squirmed. He wished for a moment that he played football like his father had. Dad had been on varsity all four years of high school, as well as an all-state quarterback. Every fall he played in a reunion game where perfect strangers slapped him on the back with admiration.

But Jacques didn't play football. He liked soccer—the feel of the ball as it smacked off the strike zone of his cleats, and the rush as he raced past the defenders, risked a shot and hit the goal clean.

Jacques picked at his food and glanced at the photograph of his mother on the dining room hutch. Her long brown hair was pulled back, and her crystal blue eyes jumped straight out at him.

Dad used to say that Mom was far and away the cutest cheerleader ever to attend Lakemont High. They had started dating junior year. Dad had gone off to college on a sports scholarship, but after a month, he broke his ankle and couldn't play football. Without the scholarship, there hadn't been enough money to keep him at school.

Mom had four brothers and two sisters. Both of her parents had worked at the Lakemont Mill, and after it closed down, she couldn't afford college either. Mom's father found a new job in Rhode Island, but when the family moved to Providence, Mom stayed behind to marry Dad. Grandmère Jeannette was happy to have Mom join her at the bridal shop, and Dad got a good job driving an eighteen-wheeler.

When Jacques was little, they'd go as a family to

watch the high school football team. Mom knew every cheer, and for homecomings, Dad wore his old team jersey.

Jacques smiled to think how his mother always yelled the loudest at the football games, but when they got back, she would take him to the park and let him kick around a soccer ball. She'd liked whatever he liked, and that's what he missed most of all.

4

The first day of school was warm and breezy. Kids greeted each other with loud whoops and high fives. Lucy and Nicole were standing with Sammy and Tim O'Shea in front of the large brick school building. Lucy had strawberry blonde hair with layered side-bangs, and her lips were always shiny. When Jacques arrived, he noticed Lucy's hazel eyes flick his way, even though she was busy admiring Nicole's new wedge sandals.

Nicole liked to match from head to toe; her nails, eye shadow and shoes were all aqua blue. She tossed her straight black hair over her shoulders whenever she was flirting, which was pretty often.

Jacques turned away from the girls and glanced around the school yard. Where were the African kids?

Boucher came by and was taking bets. "If that Mohamed dude doesn't show up today, there's no way Coach will let him play on the team."

Jacques was wondering more about the girl with the scar.

"Over there!" Sammy nudged Jacques. A van filled with Somali teenagers pulled in front of the school.

Mohamed stepped out first, followed by six boys and four girls.

"Look what they're wearing." Boucher snickered.

The Somali boys were dressed neatly—too neatly. Each boy wore tan khaki pants with a belt and collared polo shirt, all carefully tucked in. Jacques looked down at his own oversized T-shirt and cargo shorts.

As the group walked past them, Jacques mouthed, "Hey Mohamed," but the boy stared straight ahead as if he didn't see him.

The Somali girls wore ankle-length skirts and long-sleeved shirts. Large scarves were wrapped around their heads, covering their hair and shoulders. Sammy said these were called *hijabs*. Jacques couldn't imagine wearing heavy clothes like that, especially on a warm September morning. Most of the girls he knew wore shorts until November, and Nicole had been sent home last spring because her sundress didn't reach her fingertips when she held her arms straight to her sides.

Suddenly, Jacques heard a faint giggle. He found himself eye to eye with the girl from Main Street. For a split second, she looked directly into his face and grinned. She had clear white teeth, with a gap in the middle that reminded him of Grandmère Jeannette's. He saw that the jagged scar ran from the edge of her eyebrow all the way past her cheekbone. Sammy's mom said that many thousands of people had been killed in Somalia's civil war, and that sometimes boys were kidnapped to become soldiers, with girls treated even worse.

The second bell rang. Jacques grabbed his backpack and headed inside to find his room assignment. By the time he reached homeroom, the Somali girl with the bright smile and long scar was standing by the blackboard.

"Settle down, class!" Mrs. Sinclair motioned for Jacques to take his seat. "We have a new student today. Her name is Saynab, but she says that she likes to be called by her nickname, Kiki. Is that correct?" Mrs. Sinclair looked anxiously at the girl.

"Yes," the girl replied in a low soft voice, "sometimes I am calling myself Kiki."

"Kiki's family is originally from Somalia; they've recently moved here from Georgia." Mrs. Sinclair paused and glanced around the room. "Lucy and Nicole, I would like you to be Kiki's school buddies today. Please help her get settled." Gesturing toward the back, Mrs. Sinclair added, "Kiki, take that empty desk next to Jacques."

As Kiki sat down, she turned and whispered, "Hi," her round lips curling above the gap between her teeth.

Jacques couldn't remember later that day whether he said hi back or not. He hid behind his math binder while Kiki spent most of the period filling out forms in large block letters. Jacques half wished that Kiki would turn his way again, but was half afraid that she might. When the bell rang, Kiki filed out behind the other girls.

At lunch, Jacques watched Kiki go with the rest of

the Somali kids to the back of the cafeteria. The girls sat together at one table, the boys at another.

Jacques was about to sit next to Sammy and Tim O'Shea when Lucy slid over to make room. Nicole flashed thumbs-up, and Lucy started to giggle.

Nicole was breathless, as usual. "My father says the Somalis will be gone in a week! It's way too cold in Maine; they're not used to it. . . . That tall boy could hardly read! I heard he's supposed to be in eighth grade, but they're holding him back."

Jacques winced as he pushed his tray to one side. "Hey, Nicole—didn't Mrs. Sinclair tell you to go over there and help? You should ask them if they need anything."

Nicole glared back at him. "They seem just fine to me. If you want to help, be my guest."

"It looks like they're doing okay," Lucy added.

Suddenly, a voice rang out: "HEY SOMALIS! HOW DO YOU LIKE THE HAM SANDWICHES?" A girl gasped, and then the far end of the cafeteria erupted.

"What just happened?" Sammy put down his drink.

"It must be Boucher." Jacques' stomach tightened as he stood to look. "What an idiot. He should just shut up!"

Jacques felt sick. Somebody had tossed what looked like a half-eaten sandwich onto the middle of the Somali boys' table.

"What's going on?" Lucy asked. "What's wrong with ham?"

"Muslims don't eat ham, it's against their religion," Sammy replied.

"But I thought that was Jewish people." Nicole looked confused.

"Well yeah, we don't eat ham either."

Several cafeteria ladies scurried over to hush the room, but the damage was already done. Muffled snickers and "Hey, Boucher!" spread throughout the lunchroom. The Somali kids pulled back from their tables and quickly gathered their things to go.

Jacques took a deep breath and stepped forward. Maybe he should yell out that Boucher was a tool or worse, but his palms were sweaty and he felt dizzy. It seemed over already, and he needed to get to his locker before gym.

By the time Jacques reached the hallway, Kiki was standing in front of her locker a few feet away, gently kicking it. Jacques still felt dizzy. He bent over to leaf through his binders while he caught his breath. He could see Kiki trying the locker combination over and over, but it refused to open.

Lockers at Lakemont Middle School were famous for getting jammed; plenty of kids lugged their books from class to class. But Kiki didn't know this. Jacques saw that she was biting into her bottom lip. What if she started to cry? Maybe he should go apologize for the stupid way Boucher had acted.

But when Jacques glanced sideways again, he was startled by the set look on Kiki's face. She wasn't going to cry; she was simply going to get the locker open, no matter what. Kiki gave it such a sharp whack, it shocked him. What kind of trouble could a girl get into denting school property on the very first day?

Jacques rose to his feet and spun around as if noticing Kiki for the first time. In two long steps he was beside her. "What's the combination? There's a trick to it."

He jiggled his thumb against the lock while he turned the dial. It immediately popped open.

Kiki grinned. "Thanks for that."

Jacques saw that she had a dimple in the corner of her mouth just below the scar. A tiny wisp of black hair peeked out from the edge of her hijab.

A voice behind them started to boom. "My sister don't need help!"

"I was just trying to . . ." Jacques began.

"She don't need anything." Mohamed's eyes narrowed to slits.

Kiki lowered her head as Jacques shrugged and walked away. He could hear Mohamed yelling. Why in the world was Mohamed so mad? Jacques hadn't been flirting with the new girl; he'd been trying to help.

Maybe they don't want our help, he thought to himself as he headed to gym class. Was Nicole right? Was it better to just stay clear?

5

That night Jacques set two alarms, but he woke up the next morning before either went off and made it to homeroom early. With his eyes darting between his notebook and the door, he practiced saying hi under his breath. But Kiki never arrived. Mrs. Sinclair called her name out twice: "Saynab Husen," and then, "Kiki?" No answer.

Maybe that was it. Maybe the new girl was done with Lakemont Middle School. And just maybe none of the Somalis were ever coming back. But at the end of first period, Jacques saw Mohamed in the hallway, and at lunch, a group of Somali kids were sitting at the same tables as yesterday. Actually, it looked like there were even more of them this time—five or six girls, all dressed in long skirts and hijabs, and several more boys. No sign of Kiki, though.

When school let out, Jacques went to the neighbors' apartment to pick up their twin boys, Ricky and Robby. The family lived on the first floor beneath Grandmère

Jeannette's apartment, and the twins were always coming upstairs to play with Pelé. The boys were in first grade, and starting this fall, Jacques was going to get paid to watch them sometimes while their mother worked the afternoon shift at the bakery. Jacques figured he could save up enough money to buy the Arsenal jersey that he wanted so badly.

Robby chased Ricky to the park while Jacques kicked a soccer ball across the pavement. Tryouts were coming up fast. Jacques took aim at the old wooden bench at the entrance to the park. *Slam,* the ball swiftly knocked an empty soda can off the seat.

"Good shot! Do it again!" a voice squeaked. When Jacques turned, he saw a small black child standing behind him. The little boy was cheering with his hands clasped above his head. In the distance, there was Kiki, pushing a baby stroller. The baby was dressed in a blue knitted sweater and was waving a plastic truck.

"Hey," Jacques stammered, "do you live around here?"

"Oh hi." Kiki looked surprised, then kind of pleased. "We are staying in a place over there." She pointed at a dilapidated apartment building with a rickety wooden porch.

The boy hopped to the swing set where Ricky and Robby were pushing each other in the air. "You're it!" He tagged Robby and in a minute, the three children were racing around the playground, giggling.

"Is that your baby?" Jacques asked. "I mean, are these your brothers?"

"Oh yeah, the baby is called Amir. And the one who likes to talk so much—Ismail, he is nearly five."

"You weren't at school today." Jacques coughed into his elbow.

"My mother, she is looking for work, so I had to watch the little ones. I am there again tomorrow, though."

Amir threw the toy truck on the ground. Kiki leaned forward to pick it up, but Jacques reached it first. He handed it back to the squealing baby.

"And those two must be your brothers?" Kiki nodded at the twins.

"Oh . . . no," Jacques replied. "I'm babysitting; I get paid to do it. I don't have any brothers or sisters."

"That is sad." Kiki tilted her head to one side. "Why no brother, no sister?"

Jacques hesitated and then surprised himself by telling the truth: "My mom died in an accident."

Kiki nodded her head slowly. "I am sorry. For me, it is like that too—my father died in my country, before we came here."

Jacques suddenly realized that he'd never talked to any of his friends about his mother. It had been two and a half years since she'd been killed in a car crash during an April blizzard. A week later, Grandmère Jeannette had come for Easter and brought him a tiny rabbit—Pelé—in a brown wicker basket.

Kiki pulled Baby Amir from the stroller and began to sing in a low voice as she opened his bottle.

"What does it mean?" Jacques asked.

"The song?" Kiki laughed. "It is just a foolish thing we sing for babies."

"I like it." Jacques remembered how Mom would sing to him at night in her clear, sweet voice. Sometimes she and Dad would do a duet of "Frère Jacques," with Dad booming low and slightly out of tune. At Christmas they'd go caroling with families from church, and when Jacques was really little, Dad would carry him high on his shoulders, bouncing through the snowy streets while they sang.

It suddenly struck Jacques that after Mom died, they didn't go caroling anymore. He never heard his father sing off-key again.

Kiki wiped Amir's chin and put the bottle away. "I am guessing that you like Messi. Am I correct? Are you a fan?"

"What?" Jacques blinked.

"Messi, you know—the soccer star."

"He's okay . . . I guess." Jacques wondered whether Kiki could possibly know that he had three posters of Messi on his walls at home. "Why are you asking?"

"Mohamed says you are the best on the team," Kiki replied. "You will be the captain, for sure, he says."

"Your brother told you that?"

"No." Kiki smiled. "I heard him say it to my uncle."

Jacques dug his sneaker into a rut in the pavement. "Do you play?"

Kiki hesitated before answering. "In my family, girls are not supposed to play soccer like that, not really. Some girls do, but my father, he was very strict."

"You can try this out if you want to." Jacques tapped the ball in front of her.

"I don't know. . . . If Mohamed catch me, he would be angry!" Kiki squinted as she gazed past the swing set toward the edge of the playground. "My brother is not even one year older, but he watches me now as if he is the father."

"It's really okay, there's nobody around," Jacques replied.

Kiki cocked her head, pursing her lips. She still had Amir in her lap, burping as he shook the bottle.

"I can hold him." Jacques remembered how Mom used to sing and play clapping games with the babies that came into the bridal shop. He put his hands out toward Amir; it couldn't be that hard.

"I should not . . ." Kiki began, but suddenly Amir decided for them. He lunged forward, and Jacques instinctively squatted and caught him. Jacques whistled and made clucking sounds. To his amazement, Amir began to coo.

"It's no big deal, go ahead."

Kiki stood on tiptoes, shielding her dark eyes as she carefully scanned the park. Then she concentrated on the ball for a minute, taking aim. She was only wearing leather sandals, but with a firm smack, the ball soared straight and sure to the other end of the playground.

"Hey, your sister's not bad!" Jacques whispered to Amir. The baby pulled on Jacques's nose and bounced.

Every time Kiki kicked the ball, she stopped to look over her shoulder, craning her neck to search the four corners of the park. Finally, a calm look came over her face. She ran straight ahead, whacking the ball hard, pivoting and driving it forward. When Kiki jogged back, she was panting, but the gap between her teeth showed through a broad smile.

"You're good! You should go out for the girls' team."

"No." Kiki beamed. "This is not true. I am no good at soccer, and my English is terrible too."

"You speak really well! How'd you learn?" Jacques asked.

Kiki sat and rubbed her foot. "When we left my country, we came first to a place near Atlanta. We stayed there almost a year, and I had a good teacher."

"What was her name?"

"Her name was Kiki."

"Seriously?" Jacques looked up.

"In Somalia, it was not always safe to go to school, and I had to help at home. When we got to America, I was behind in every subject. My teacher's family came from Africa. She understood my situation and was very kind to me. Now I like to remember her, so I use the nickname." Kiki smiled. "It makes things easier, you know?"

"I get it," Jacques replied. "I was named after my grandfather—but sometimes, kids just call me Jack."

"Hey, you are not too bad with babies." Amir was resting his head on Jacques's shoulder. Kiki scooped her brother into her arms, but Amir reached back and grabbed Jacques's hair.

"Ouch, this little man is strong!" Jacques grinned.

Ricky and Ismail ran over, with Robby three steps behind: "We're starving!"

"I got something in here." Kiki pulled out two triangle-shaped pastries and divided them among the open mouths. "You want to try?" She held out a piece for Jacques. "Hooyo made it this morning."

The pastry was filled with spicy meat mixed with onions.

Kiki laughed when she saw the expression on Jacques's face. "It is called *sambusa*. They are like your hot dogs—we eat them all the time."

A loud rustling noise came from the other end of the playground.

"Hey, Gagnon!"

Jacques's stomach flipped. Duane and another teenage boy were standing by the fence. A blonde girl was tucked under Duane's shoulder. When she turned slightly, Jacques took another look and blinked. Monique! What was she doing with Duane? Was it possible she was actually marrying that creep?

Kiki quickly stuffed the rest of the food in her bag and yelled for Ismail. Her lips were set together and her brow was pinched.

"Hold on a minute. . . ." Jacques began, but Kiki was already jogging behind the stroller without looking back. Ismail ran after her.

Jacques wiped the last bit of sambusa from his hands as the older boys came close.

Monique waited by the fence alone.

"Who's the Somali babe?" Duane put his hands in his pockets.

"Nobody." Jacques's pulse began to race. What if Duane still had the knife? "Just a girl from school."

"We have a little job for you," the other boy sneered. He was slightly shorter, with a soft, full belly. Two small silver hoops hung from one earlobe.

"I'm watching these kids." Jacques shook his head. "I can't talk."

"Don't mess with us." Duane leaned over Jacques's shoulder. "Garth and I need your help."

"I've got to go!" Jacques motioned to the twins. He grabbed Robby by the elbow, pulling him toward the gate while Ricky scurried after them.

"You forgot the ball," Ricky shouted.

"Leave it." Jacques bounded ahead. "We'll get it later."

When Jacques finally stopped to let the twins catch their breath, the older boys and Monique had vanished.

6

Jacques dropped Ricky and Robby with their mother and raced up the stairs to Grandmère Jeannette's apartment. When he stepped inside, he was shocked to find his grandmother slumped over the dining room table.

"Grandmère! What's wrong?" Her head lifted, and Jacques exhaled sharply. But he could see that her eyes were red and swollen. "Are you sick?"

"It's nothing; I didn't hear you come in." Grandmère Jeannette wiped her face and pushed up from the table. "I'll go fix you somethin' to eat."

"No," Jacques said. "Tell me what happened."

Trembling, Grandmère Jeannette fell back into the chair. A stack of official looking papers were piled high in front of her.

"What are those?"

Grandmère Jeannette shook her head. "The bank wants to take the shop," she finally answered.

"Our shop? The bridal shop?" Jacques could barely move his lips.

Slow and silent, Grandmère Jeannette nodded yes.

"I don't understand. You've had that place forever!"

When Jacques was little, they'd moved around a lot. But the bridal shop was always there—in some ways, it felt the most like home. Mom had taken Jacques to work with her nearly every Saturday. They'd stop along the way at the library, and Jacques would curl up in the corner of the office with a pile of books while Mom and Grandmère Jeannette sold gowns. By the time he was six or seven, Jacques could help out by sweeping or picking up pins from the sewing room floor.

After Mom died, Jacques continued going to the shop to help his grandmother. Sometimes, it even seemed like Mom was still there. Upstairs in the office or behind the curtains of the dressing room, Jacques could almost hear her voice softly humming, "Frère Jacques."

They couldn't lose the bridal shop.

"The bank don't care that it's been near twenty years. Or that your grandfather's heart gave out trying to build up the business. I've got no money for the mortgage." Grandmère Jeannette looked exhausted. Deep lines drooped down the sides of her mouth.

"Dad's working now—he can help."

"Your father lost his job two weeks ago," Grandmère Jeannette said quietly.

Jacques felt like he'd been kicked. "He got fired?"

"They promised they'd call him back in a couple months, but I don't think we can count on it." Grandmère Jeannette looked away, and her voice began to waver. "If I lose the shop, I don't know how we'd make ends meet. I couldn't bear to make you leave this apartment." She wiped her nose with a crumpled tissue.

"I have some babysitting money. You can have it." Jacques pulled out the ten dollars the twins' mother had just given him.

"You hold onto that. You'll be needin' it for college someday." Grandmère Jeannette squeezed Jacques's hand. "If we can just get through 'til Christmas, I could turn things around with the extra holiday business—I know I could."

"Dad can find something else, maybe truck driving again."

"You don't need to be the one worrying, *mon cher.* You surprised me, or I wouldn't have told you."

The phone began to ring, and Jacques leaned over to answer.

"Hello?" There was silence on the other end, but he could hear someone breathing. Then the phone went dead.

"Prank call." Jacques's stomach was turning.

"Hold on a minute." Grandmère Jeannette tapped her forehead. "I nearly forgot. Somebody called here a little while ago lookin' for you. An older boy, I guess."

The sick feeling in Jacques's stomach spread up to

his chest, making it hard to breath. "What was the kid's name?"

"He wouldn't say—just that he'd see you soon enough." After blowing her nose, Grandmère Jeannette shuffled into the kitchen.

Jacques checked to see that the front door was bolted shut. He went into his bedroom and slammed his fist into his hand. How could Dad have lost another job? Why hadn't he said anything about it? Jacques ran his fingers through his hair, opened the closet door and stood tall in front of the mirror.

"I'm not taking any of your bull, Duane!" Jacques watched his reflection carefully. The orange freckles on his cheeks seemed to pop out. Long brown curls fell into his eyes, and his lips were twitching. Try again. This time, he crossed his arms in front of his chest: "You're crazy to think you can get away with it! You're gonna end up back in jail!" Crap, he still looked ridiculous.

"Were you calling me?" Grandmère Jeannette was knocking.

"I'm fine." Jacques opened the door a crack. "I was practicing something for school."

"One more thing . . ." Grandmère Jeannette hesitated. "You don't go sayin' nothin' about this to your father, okay? It's hard enough on him."

"I can help more in the shop; I promise."

"I just wish your dear *maman* was still here," Grandmère Jeannette said softly. "She was the finest part of him. Donny's never been the same without her."

Jacques's eyes stung as he felt his grandmother's hand touch his cheek. After she left, he went and took one last look in the mirror.

"How much money do I get if I say yes?" he whispered.

7

The next morning Kiki rushed into homeroom two minutes late. Jacques felt his face go hot as she flashed him a silent "hi." When Kiki fumbled for a pen, Jacques reached into his backpack and pulled out three Sharpies for her to choose from. One of her books slipped off the desk, and Jacques dove to the floor to catch it.

When he picked himself off the floor, he noticed Lucy staring at him. At lunch, she seemed mad. "You're in my way." She bumped her backpack into Jacques's shoulder.

"Hey!" He rubbed his arm. "I need to be in one piece for soccer tryouts today."

"I don't think you've got much of a chance, anyhow," Lucy replied. "I guess that was kind of mean," she added, slamming him in the other shoulder.

"You think?" Sammy smirked.

"Did you see the Somali kids playing at recess yesterday?" O'Shea seemed to be missing the drama. "That Mohamed dude could go professional! He's amazing."

"Thanks a lot." Jacques gathered his stuff to go.

"Just sayin' . . ." O'Shea shrugged.

"C'mon." Sammy stood and motioned to Jacques. As they walked out of the lunchroom he whispered, "They're idiots. And Lucy is plain jealous. She thinks you like Kiki."

"That's crazy. . . ." Jacques was cut off by the sight of Mohamed striding past him and staring straight ahead. He looked six foot four at least.

When school let out, Jacques noticed that the wind had picked up. His long-distance shot was his trademark—a wide smack, and the ball would arch above the goalie's head and spin into the goal. But wind was a funny thing, as Coach liked to say. It could throw off anybody's game.

By the time he got to practice, Jacques's head was throbbing, and his shoulder felt stiff. Mohamed looked even taller and sharper as he sailed along the edge of the field. He was good at defense, midfield and offense—there was nothing this kid couldn't do.

"Get out there, all of you! Let's see what you got." Coach Morrin's eyes were watery from the breeze, and he blew his nose with a loud honk.

Jacques ran the ball down the field, faked to the left, and after a gust of wind, placed the ball in. It soared over O'Shea's head into the sweet spot. Sammy flashed thumbs-up. Jacques jumped in triumph a split second before realizing that Mohamed was coming up fast from behind. Mohamed danced with the ball, skipping it between his legs, left and right and then just as a blast of air hit them—*slam!*—straight like a bullet the ball swooshed right into the goal. It was horrible and beautiful. Jacques could see Boucher shaking his head and making a chopping motion across his own neck.

Jacques scored three goals with two assists, but Mohamed made five perfect goals. Jacques jogged back to the edge of the field, spent. He was beat, and he knew it.

"I'll post results on the door of the gym tomorrow." Coach Morrin rubbed the back of his neck. "That wind was real strong today; you guys did okay, considering."

Jacques and Sammy walked home in silence. When it was time for Sammy to veer off, he cleared his throat like he was starting to say something, but Jacques shrugged and walked away.

Rounding the corner by Grandmère Jeannette's, Jacques spotted a ball of white fur hopping across the front yard toward the road. He froze and drew a sharp breath. Pelé! How in the world had he gotten out? In a split second, Jacques heard the ear-shattering roar of a broken muffler coming fast from up the street, and that was when everything went into slow motion. Jacques couldn't remember later whether he saw the Harley motorcycle first or just heard its thundering engine. He dug into the pavement and sprinted. The rest came in flashes: Pelé, Ricky running toward the road, the black van speeding forward. Harley driver swearing, swerving, skidding. And then a girl in a flowing green skirt running up the street, screaming and waving her arms.

The screech, the bang, the honking as the motorcycle jumped and hit the edge of the sidewalk, spinning around him. Cursing, followed by darkness.

"You okay? You okay?" Someone was shaking his shoulder.

Jacques blinked, and closed his eyes again. Was he dead? Was this a dream? He opened one lid, looking straight into Kiki's face. Ricky stood beside her, red-cheeked and crying.

"I'm sorry! I'm sorry! I'm sorry!" Ricky panted.

"What happened?" Jacques groaned. "Where's Pelé?" He propped himself up on his elbow, but his head felt light. The Harley driver revved its engine and roared away in a cloud of dust, honking and swearing. The van was gone too. The street was empty.

"That crazy guy nearly hit you!" Kiki's voice was hoarse. "Are you okay? Did you hurt anything?"

"You saved Pelé!" Robby held the bunny against Jacques's cheek as Jacques struggled to sit up.

"Are you hurt?" Kiki repeated, breathless.

Jacques shook his head. He wasn't sure yet, but he didn't think so. He sat in the middle of the street, his heart pounding against soft fur.

Ricky tried to explain. "Your grandma said we could take Pelé outside, and Robby was supposed to be watching, but I kicked the ball under the bushes, and we had to find it." He stopped to wipe his nose on the back of a grimy hand. "When we came back, Pelé was gone!"

"Can you walk? You better get out of the road before another car comes." Kiki looked anxiously up and down the street.

"What are you doing here?" Jacques muttered as he pulled himself to his feet.

"I was on my way to the library to get help with math. But then I saw the motorbike, and it was coming at Ricky so quick . . . and I started to run, but you got there first." Kiki's strained expression melted into a crooked grin. "You *are* really fast. No wonder my brother says so."

Jacques hobbled to the yard and collapsed on the grass. Oblivious to near disaster, the bunny began to purr.

Jacques gave the boys a weak high five. "You keep Pelé out back next time, okay?"

Robby tugged on Ricky's sleeve. "It's almost supper." The twins ran into the house while Kiki knelt on the grass.

She pointed to the bruise on Jacques's leg. "This looks bad."

"It's just a little sore, that's all," Jacques said. "I guess I'm lucky it happened *after* soccer tryouts."

"Oh yes," Kiki replied. "Mohamed was all nervous about it when he left for school this morning."

Mohamed? Nervous? Was that possible? Jacques rubbed the bruised knee. "I don't know why he'd be worried. Your brother is super good, like totally amazing."

Kiki sighed. "They had a special team in Atlanta. There was a man there, a coach who spoke to

Mohamed about trying out, and maybe he could be, you know, a professional player someday." Kiki stroked Pelé's long silky ears. "But Hooyo, she wanted to move here because my uncle had already come to Maine. So Mohamed lost his chance."

"That's too bad," Jacques said. "Maybe he can still do it. He could play at college someday. You too."

Kiki shrugged. "I don't know if I am ever getting to college. I could not understand my math sheet, not at all."

"I'm pretty good with numbers." Jacques nodded toward the backpack sitting next to Kiki.

She hesitated, twirling the edge of her hijab. "Maybe I better go; I am supposed to make dinner."

"It's just like school here—it's fine," Jacques replied. "We can hang out for another minute. Nobody will care." Jacques handed Pelé to Kiki, picked up her math binder and quickly showed her how to do the homework.

"You are like a math wizard," Kiki said. "You know it better than the teacher."

"Miss Woodhouse is half crazy. She's been at school at least a hundred years. My dad had her." Jacques stood and picked up the soccer ball. "Watch this."

Kiki giggled while Jacques set the ball in front of Pelé. The rabbit sniffed, then hopped forward, pushing the ball back and forth toward the house with his nose.

"He thinks that bush is the goal," Jacques explained. "Look at him tuck it away."

Kiki laughed. "He is a striker! He is going to make

the team for sure." She rose and picked up her backpack. "Mohamed must be home by now. Thanks for the help. I will see you at school."

Jacques bent forward to lift up Pelé, and that's when he noticed a guy in a gray hoodie and sagging gym pants jogging down the street away from him. Jacques couldn't see his face, but he knew exactly who was there.

Jacques pulled Pelé close to his chest. "You better keep your distance, Duane!" he hissed under his breath. "I'm warning you."

8

There was a note on the gym door the next morning written in black swirling script that didn't look anything like Coach's handwriting.

Tim O'Shea read the words aloud: "Coach Out Sick. No Practice."

"What the heck!" Boucher exclaimed. "What about soccer tryouts? Who made the team?"

"I guess we'll just have to wait 'til tomorrow," Jacques replied. Thank you, God, he added silently.

Jacques picked up his backpack and cut through the boys still hanging by the door. Mohamed must be so sure of himself; he hadn't even shown up.

Sammy caught up with Jacques by the lockers. "You been asked to the Sadie Hawkins yet?"

"What?" Jacques frowned.

"Sadie Hawkins. The dance. Girls ask the boys. It's this weekend."

"No," Jacques said. "And it sounds stupid."

"Right." Sammy's face got kind of red. "But the thing is, Nicole just asked me, so I guess I'm gonna go."

"Didn't you say you hated her guts?" Jacques asked.

"That was last week." Sammy's braces gleamed in a sheepish grin.

Kiki was walking toward them. "How is your knee?" She smiled, but kept her eyes to the floor and didn't slow down.

"Fine," Jacques mumbled.

"What was that about?" Sammy asked.

"Nothing."

"She can't ask you to the dance," Sammy said. "I doubt she can even go to the dance. They're not allowed. Muslim boys and girls don't hang out together 'til they are, like, married."

"We're just friends," Jacques quickly responded. He scanned the hallway, wondering where Mohamed was.

At lunch, Lucy stormed past their regular table and banged her backpack down next to three cheerleaders. Her cheeks were flushed, and she wouldn't look Jacques's way.

"What's up with her?" Jacques asked.

Sammy and O'Shea burst out laughing.

With Coach Morrin sick and practice called off, Jacques figured he'd go surprise Grandmère Jeannette after school. He broke away fast, hoping to avoid running into anyone, especially Mohamed. Two blocks from school, though, he bumped smack into Father Lazar, stepping out from the Save-and-Shop.

"Oh, hi, Father," Jacques stammered. He suddenly realized that he hadn't been to confession all summer.

"Jacques." The priest smiled warmly. "I was just thinking about you."

"You were?" Crap, maybe it had been a whole year since confession.

"Yes, indeed. Jeannette mentioned that you play basketball."

"Basketball?" Jacques blinked. "What I mean is— soccer is more my game."

"I'm sure you are skilled at both, but we don't have a soccer field in the church hall." Father Lazar chuckled. "Here's what I want to talk to you about: The clergy in town have been brainstorming about how to welcome our new African neighbors. We've decided to hold a family night this Saturday, with a basketball game for the teens." Father Lazar paused. "It would mean a lot if you could come."

Jacques shifted his feet. "There's kind of a dance this weekend at school. Sadie Hawkins."

"I see," Father Lazar replied.

"I might get invited by this girl. . . ."

"I understand," the priest said.

But Jacques wasn't exactly sure that he did.

"You think about it. If you change your mind, bring some kids with you. They don't have to be church members—all comers welcome. The ladies are planning an impressive dessert table, did I mention that already?"

Jacques waved goodbye with a few grunts about having to help his grandmother. He sprinted the rest of the way to the shop, cutting through the alley behind Main Street. Mr. Silverstein, the owner of the Army Navy Store, was out back heaving empty boxes onto the curb.

"Do you need help?" Jacques saw that the biggest box was hard for the older man to carry.

"Oh hello there, Jacques." Mr. Silverstein smiled. "Thank you, but I've got it. How's your grandmother been doing? How's business?"

"It's maybe been a little slow, I guess," Jacques replied.

Mr. Silverstein sighed as he dropped the last box onto the curb. "There's not much traffic on Main Street these days. Too many people are out of work, and nobody's got money to spend." He hesitated for a moment as he cleared his throat. "Tell me something. Your grandmother, does she go out much on weekends?"

"What do you mean?" Jacques asked. He eyeballed Mr. Silverstein closely. He was a tall, trim man with gray hair that grew thick behind the ears, but not so much on the top of his head. He was sixty at least, Jacques decided.

"Well, does she, er . . . ever see people?"

Jacques wasn't sure what to say. "Sometimes she likes going to the speedway, and, um, Grandmère always goes to church on Sundays."

"Interesting—church and racing cars." Mr. Silverstein smiled as he turned away. "You won't tell her that I was asking, now will you?"

"Definitely not," Jacques answered.

Jacques walked along the curb to the back entrance of the bridal shop. Afternoon sun streamed through the display windows, and he could see girls from a large wedding party admiring themselves in the three-way mirror. The girls were all shapes, all ages and all sizes; the bride was short and not slim.

"You give yourself a good twirl." Grandmère Jeannette took one of the bridesmaids and spun her around in the mirror. "Look how the fancy pleats on the backside make you look like a model!" Jeannette swerved, diving toward a taller bridesmaid. "You ought to be wearing heels with that dress; the higher the better—the lace on the hemline shows off those gorgeous legs you got."

The tall girl giggled with appreciation as Grandmère Jeannette leaned forward to claim her prize. She pulled the bride to the center of the group and asked her to step on a small wooden stand. Grandmère Jeannette fluffed the back of the gown and arranged the train so the stand didn't show. With a triumphant flourish, she placed an eyelet veil over the bride's long wavy hair.

"Now look, perfection! Your wedding photo!" Grandmère Jeannette made clicking noises as if she was taking lots of pictures.

She's amazing! Jacques thought. Just like a soccer star, dribbling it home.

"I look so beautiful. . . ." There were actual tears in the bride's eyes. Her mother was pulling out tissues. The sale was done.

Grandmère Jeannette licked her lips as she took their deposit. "My handsome grandson," she announced, pointing her pinkie in Jacques's direction.

"Tres beau!" The mother of the bride nodded.

After the women left, Grandmère Jeannette collapsed on the couch with a satisfied grunt. "What are you doing here this afternoon? Don't you have soccer?"

"I came to help," Jacques replied. "Practice got cancelled."

"Good timing," Grandmère Jeannette said. "It's been busy and we need every sale. Why don't you make some boxes and put those dresses away."

Another bridal party arrived for a fitting. Grandmère Jeannette took them to the sewing room, but the front door quickly opened again, and a not-so-young lady wearing sparkling gold eye shadow above thick false lashes walked inside.

"My grandmother will only be a minute," Jacques said.

The woman ignored him. She went to the rack filled with formal gowns and shuffled through a few before turning to go.

"Did you find your size okay?" Jacques asked.

"Well, sweetie—I'm kind of in a rush, and I'm looking for something special."

"Do you need a wedding gown?" It didn't seem likely.

The woman laughed, her large lips parting. "No, I need a dress for my act. I'm a dancer at a club in Portland. I'm looking for something exotic . . . but classy, of course." The woman's teeth were whiter than any teeth Jacques had ever seen—whiter than Grandmère Jeannette's best china that she only brought out for Easter.

"We have lots of cool gowns." Jacques went over to the dress rack.

"It's fine, I can look for myself." The woman seemed dubious.

"You should try this one, for sure." Jacques handed her a pink satin gown with sequins and silver beads stitched to one strap. "I think it's your size."

"You're cute." The woman stopped and checked the tag. "I suppose it can't hurt to try this on." The woman paused before entering the dressing booth. "What else you got?"

For dinner that night, Grandmère Jeannette served pork ragout with garlic mashed potatoes. "*Mon Dieu, our Jacques made three sales! Full price!*" Grandmère Jeannette clapped her hands while Jacques felt his face turn as pink as the dress he'd sold. "I was out back, and I didn't even hear the first lady come in."

Dad grunted and dug at his dinner. He drained a can of beer and crushed it with one hand.

When Grandmère Jeannette went into the kitchen to get dessert, Dad turned to Jacques. "I know what she told you. I'll find some other work, okay? You don't need to be busting your head about it."

"It was nothing!" Jacques replied quickly.

Dad rose, his fork clattering to the floor.

Jacques's stomach tightened. He was doing his best; why was Dad angry? When Jacques was little, whenever Dad would get heated up about something, Mom would tilt her head and say, "Put away your grizzly bear, darling!" Dad would nearly always stop his fuming, take Mom in his arms and do a fake growl until they both started laughing.

"You want some, Donny?" Grandmère Jeannette held a Maple Sugar Pie in front of them.

Dad didn't answer. He left the table, and a moment later, they heard the front door slam.

"Don't worry." Grandmère Jeannette set the pie down. "Enjoy your food. He'll be back soon." She pointed the pie cutter toward the ceiling. "You did great today. Your *maman* would be proud—real proud."

Jacques closed his eyes, trying to hold on to the memory of Mom wrapped in Dad's big bear arms. He didn't feel like pie anymore, but he ate two slices anyway.

9

"Watch out for the lobsters—they bite!" Boucher snickered as he strode past Kiki's desk. A fleet of buses had arrived to take the entire seventh grade to Spruce Point Beach for a field trip, followed by an afternoon at the amusement park on the pier. Kids were yelling and hopping in the air like pogo sticks while Mrs. Sinclair tried to bring the noise down to a dull roar.

Jacques saw the question mark lingering on Kiki's face. "Ignore Boucher! It's the best day of school."

"I never seen the ocean yet," Kiki said. "In Somalia, my family lived far away from the sea."

When they got to the beach, kids leaped from the buses and ran toward the dunes, but Kiki lagged behind. A silver mist hung over the ocean. Sunlight peeked through fat gray clouds. At the far end of the beach, Jacques could make out the silhouette of an old lighthouse, appearing and disappearing into a blanket of fog.

"Come on!" Jacques yelled.

Kiki pulled off her sandals and jumped on the beach. Laughing in surprise as her toes sank into the soft sand, she twirled on one foot, her hijab billowing behind her as she raced toward the sea.

Tim O'Shea whistled. "That girl can run."

"You should see her kick." Jacques grinned.

When Kiki reached the water, she kept on going. She splashed a few feet into the edge of a spent wave, stopped short and pivoted, shock etched on her face.

"It's freezing!" Kiki ran back out, the bottom of her skirt dripping. "What kind of crazy ocean is this?"

"We're in Maine!" Jacques laughed.

Mrs. Sinclair divided the kids into teams of four. Jacques, Lucy, Kiki and Sammy had half an hour to find some living creatures.

"How about out there?" Kiki started walking in the direction of a jetty where a long wall of boulders jutted into the water.

"It's covered in seaweed." Lucy looked unsure.

Kiki began climbing to the top. Balancing on the balls of her bare feet, she hopped from rock to rock. The others followed, but the seaweed and barnacles made it hard going.

"Ouch!" Lucy tripped on a slab of granite.

Jacques reached forward to pull her up. He felt a strange jolt as Lucy's warm fingers clung to his wrist. Her pony tail was loose, and damp ringlets framed her face.

"I'm going back." She frowned. "You coming?"

Jacques hesitated, the weird electricity still tingling in his fingertips.

Then he shook his head, no, and gestured for Sammy to keep up with him. Nearly all the rocks this far out were topped with green slime. Jacques slowed down as a roll of fog came in, obscuring the end of the jetty.

"Where's Kiki? Do you see her?" Sammy craned his neck.

Jacques's pulse began to race. He turned in every direction and strained to listen, but all he could hear were the waves slapping against stone. What if Kiki fell into the ocean? Did she even know how to swim?

"Kiki?" he called out.

His words hung empty in the fog.

"Kiki! Kiki! Where are you?" Jacques shouted.

Suddenly, she bobbed up from the side of a boulder with a sand dollar in her hand. "Is it still alive?" Kiki flipped the shell in her palm to admire the delicate flower pattern on top. "It is beautiful."

Jacques released a long breath and looked closely at the sand dollar. He'd seen a hundred of them, maybe a thousand, but Kiki was right—the flower design on the shell, with its round symmetrical petals, was amazing.

Kiki's eyes were shining, reflecting water and the sun.

"Yeah." Jacques examined the outline of the star and mouth hole on the bottom. "That *is* cool."

By the time they returned to the beach, Mrs. Sinclair was halfway through a lecture on jellyfish.

"Spineless—like you, Gagnon!" Boucher hissed. He covered his face with his elbow, cackling.

A million things to shout back ran through Jacques's mind, but what was the use? If he started something with Boucher, it was going to end in a fight, and he'd probably be the one to get in trouble, maybe even miss the afternoon at the pier. It just wasn't worth it. Jacques could see Kiki looking his way, her mouth slightly open, expecting him to do something. He glanced up at the sky, down at his feet and kicked at the sand.

Finally, Mrs. Sinclair handed out free tickets for the rides.

"Hey, Kiki! You're gonna love The Dominator—it's *sick*!" Boucher gestured toward the enormous roller coaster rocketing above them. As he spoke, the cart at the top of the ride descended in a perpendicular roar.

"Yes, why not?" Kiki crossed her arms and stared straight at Boucher.

Boucher flinched and turned to Jacques. "What's the matter, Gagnon? You look scared!" Without waiting for an answer, he tore off toward the ride.

"You sure you want to go on that?" Sammy asked Jacques in a low voice. "Last time, you chucked."

"That was fifth grade," Jacques replied, "and you don't need to remind me."

"You can come with us." Nicole motioned to Kiki as the girls walked toward the roller coaster. The line was short, and they quickly stepped forward to the very front cart. Kiki stopped and smoothed her skirt, then climbed in between Lucy and Nicole.

"Hold on a minute." The attendant pointed at Jacques. "There's room for one more."

"Me?" Jacques croaked.

Lucy giggled as Jacques squeezed in beside her. Kiki's face was blank, but Jacques noticed that the edge of her nose was twitching. She stared ahead at the empty track and sky. When the attendant flipped the switch, the cart lurched forward.

Jacques could feel Lucy's breath coming in and out next to him, or maybe it was his own chest heaving. He tried to focus on the *ricky-tick-tick* of the cogs as the cart rose above the ground. The early morning mist had cleared. You could see the ocean, the beach, the lighthouse. Not so bad, Jacques thought for a moment. Then the cart teetered at the very top and plunged in a free fall toward the ocean. Jacques shut his eyes and gritted his teeth, trying hard not to faint. His stomach rose into his throat, and his hands gripped the bar, fingernails scratching icy metal.

They swerved to the left, and Jacques felt Lucy clutch his arm, her body leaning into his shoulder. She smelled like flowers. The wind came rushing against his face so hard that he couldn't open his eyes. His stomach heaved and flipped as the cart dropped again.

When Jacques finally managed to blink, he could see the girls leaning forward, arms high above their heads, screaming and laughing as they flew toward the bottom with a wild screech.

And then it was over. The cart slid to a stop, but Jacques's stomach was still in motion.

Boucher was hanging over the fence. "Took you long enough!"

Just don't pass out in front of him, Jacques thought. Or Kiki. Or Lucy. Anything but that.

Sammy jumped out from behind. "You okay?"

"I'm fine," Jacques mumbled. But he wasn't. His head felt light, and he could taste the hot dogs from lunch in his throat.

"I gotta puke!" Jacques stumbled toward the nearest trash can.

"Go Gagnon!" Boucher cackled. "How about another turn?"

"Shut it, Boucher!" Sammy exclaimed under his breath. He stood beside Jacques, blocking him with his body and trying hard not to look.

Jacques rose and wiped his mouth on his sleeve. "Did the girls see me?"

"No way," Sammy quickly replied. Jacques knew he was lying.

Jacques scanned the grounds. Kiki, Lucy and Nicole were standing in front of the cotton candy machine, giggling. Kiki said something that made the other girls double over in hysterics. Her eyes met Jacques's, and she turned and walked toward him.

"Here, maybe this can make you feel better." Kiki held out a mound of pink fluff. The edge of the scar crinkled when she smiled.

Jacques shook his head. "I'm good for now . . . but thanks."

Kiki licked a dab of cotton candy off her lips and grinned. This time, the gap between her teeth was filled in bright pink.

10

On Thursday morning the soccer team list was finally tacked to the gym door. Next to the list, a cardboard poster was decorated in blue and yellow flowers. In large block letters, it said Girls Don't Wait! Ask Your Date.

Jacques walked by the team list twice before taking a look. He exhaled when he saw his name halfway down the list; though the truth was, it didn't look as if Coach Morrin had cut anybody.

Then Jacques's eyesight went blurry. Rubbing his forehead, he inched closer. Toward the bottom of the sheet in bold letters he read the word CO-CAPTAINS. Underneath there were two names: *Mohamed Husen,* and just below it, *Jacques Gagnon.*

Co-captains! Jacques wasn't sure whether to shout or be sick. What was Coach thinking? How in the world was he going to lead the team alongside a boy who seemed to hate him?

Sammy came up from behind. "It's not fair. You should be the only captain. Just you."

"No." Jacques's head dropped. "Let's face it; I'm lucky Coach even made me co-captain this year."

Lucy was walking down the hall toward them, her arms filled with books and binders. Sammy grinned and slipped away in the other direction.

"Hey!" Lucy stopped and spun one toe against the floor. She was wearing blue denim shorts with lace pockets hanging out; her hair was gathered in a butter-fly clip.

"Oh hi," Jacques responded.

"The roller coaster at Spruce Point Beach was awe-some, wasn't it?" Lucy gazed into his face and smiled.

"Guess so," Jacques replied cautiously. Was she making fun of him?

"I was kind of wondering—are you going to the dance?" Lucy stretched high on her toes.

She's taller than I am, Jacques noted. "What dance?"

Jacques's eyes slid down to the binder in Lucy's arms. On its spine, there was a red Sharpie heart with the initial "J" in the center.

When Lucy saw where he was looking, she quickly moved her hand to cover the spot. "I'm talking about the Sadie Hawkins dance this weekend."

"Actually . . . " Jacques coughed. "Actually, there's something really important I need to do. Father Lazar wants me to come to church. They're having a party to welcome the African families."

"Oh really." Lucy's left eyebrow began to twitch. "You're saying that you have to go to church on Saturday night?"

"Yeah," Jacques said. "Father Lazar is kind of making me. Lots of kids are going. You can come if you want."

"I'll think about it," Lucy replied flatly. She wrapped her arms around her books and backed away. She wasn't smiling anymore.

Sammy caught up with Jacques in front of homeroom. "Did Lucy ask you?"

"I guess so." Jacques sighed.

"What'd you say?"

"I told her I had to go to church." Jacques caught the mangled expression on Sammy's lips. "It was all I could think of! I told her you were going too."

"What?" Sammy's jaw dropped before they both cracked up. "Well, I'm not going to the dance, either. Nicole just told me that she asked someone else."

"You're kidding!" Jacques exclaimed. "Who's the dude?"

"Boucher. Apparently, she's going out with him, starting this morning."

"Good thing you didn't like her." Jacques smirked.

"Are you kidding?" Sammy snorted. "I *never* liked her! I was just being—polite."

"Grandmère's making blueberry crumble and whoopie pies for the church party." Jacques patted his stomach.

"Count me in." Sammy grinned.

II

Confirmation, confession, cub scouts . . . and Mass
every Sunday. Jacques had been to St. Francis at least
once a week for most of his life. The church was the biggest building in Lakemont, and you could see its soar-
ing spires from almost any place in town. Attached to
the stone sanctuary, there was a more ordinary-looking
meeting hall and gym. Lots of clubs, like the Boy
Scouts, met at St. Francis; Jacques usually felt as comfortable there as in Grandmère Jeannette's living room.

But not tonight. Jacques fiddled with the keys in
his pocket as he walked over to the church party with
Sammy. Grandmère Jeannette had left early to help set
up. He knew that Ricky and Robby were going because
their mom had asked if they could take along Pelé;
apparently some of the younger kids were bringing pets
to share. He wasn't sure who else would be there. He
half wondered whether the Somali families would even
come.

Father Lazar stood at the church door fidgeting

with his collar, but his face lit up when he saw the boys. "Jacques, I'm delighted to see you! Truly delighted! And I'm glad you brought a friend." The priest pumped Sammy's hand, up and down, several times. "The basketball game is just starting. Some boys from the high school team are here, so it ought to be lively."

In the social hall Jacques recognized several older ladies arranging food platters. There were a few Somali families, mostly women and small children, sitting on bridge chairs. The Somali women wore floor-length *baati* dresses, with large flowered patterns. Their hair and shoulders were covered with scarves or longer hijabs.

Sister Bernadette, the oldest nun in Lakemont, was settled on a bench in the corner. She wore an old-fashioned black habit. Sister Bernadette had dressed that way for so long that Jacques hadn't really noticed. Now it seemed strange to see her sitting next to African women who also kept their heads covered.

A high-pitched squeal made him turn. Baby Amir was squirming in the arms of a lady who looked so much like Kiki that Jacques did a double take, but he knew that it had to be Kiki's mother. She was pretty like her daughter, with large brown eyes and the same gap between her teeth, although the woman had no scar.

Then a girl in a long print dress and green hijab reached for the baby, and Jacques's heart began to thump. He thought Kiki noticed him, too, but she didn't look up. Amir lifted one pudgy hand in his direction and sucked his fingers on the other.

Sammy nudged Jacques toward the gym. Father Lazar had recruited three of the biggest guys from the high school varsity team. They towered above everyone else. The ceiling of the gym wasn't that high, and the basket was placed a little lower than regulation. The high school boys could dunk without trying.

"Come join our side!" A senior with flaming red hair handed Jacques and Sammy basketball jerseys.

Jacques recognized a Somali boy from school. Tim O'Shea and two dudes from science class were playing too. O'Shea pumped a fist in greeting.

Just then, Mohamed walked into the gym. Jacques froze as he took a spot on the other team. Mohamed was nearly as tall as the high school boys and every bit as muscular.

The ref blew the whistle, and the high school guys tipped off. They were good, but Jacques couldn't keep his eyes off Mohamed.

Mohamed wasn't especially skilled at basketball. He immediately got called for traveling. When it was Jacques's turn to guard him, it wasn't that hard. He was taller, of course, but he hesitated whenever he got the ball.

Time was running out in the third quarter. O'Shea passed the ball to Mohamed, but he was so far down the court that Jacques relaxed and turned away a split second before the buzzer went off. Out of the corner of his eyes, he saw Mohamed send the ball up for a Hail Mary lob. It was a wild, hopeless throw, and Jacques was already heading back, when the crowd gathered on the sidelines began to holler. The ball swooshed right in. From beyond half-court. Incredible.

"Did that just happen?" The boy with red hair slapped his knee. "That kid told me he's never played ball before."

"Ever?" O'Shea and Sammy both gasped.

"Only pick-up games in the park." The boy shook his head.

And then Jacques saw something he hadn't seen before. For a minute, Mohamed stretched his arms behind his back and smiled.

Mohamed put up two rebounds in the fourth quarter, but both missed. Jacques watched him push off from his left foot, and suddenly it struck him: "He's a lefty. . . ."

"What?" Sammy mouthed from across the court.

Jacques tapped his left arm, but Sammy didn't get it.

Jacques and Sammy's team won easily, forty to twenty-six. The boys slapped palms with the opposing team, but when they came face to face, Mohamed looked away.

Back in the social hall, Jacques saw Ricky and Robby sitting cross-legged with Pelé under a large banner: Pet the Rabbit, Fifty Cents. Money to Help New Mainers. Six or seven other kids sat sprawled nearby with their assorted kittens, puppies, gerbils and signs.

Most of the Somali families were seated at the folding tables, chatting quietly. A few more church members and other people had arrived, but they stood on the opposite side of the room.

Suddenly, Jacques saw Kiki's little brother dart across the social hall and plunk down beside the twins. Ismail was wearing a Ninja Turtles sweatshirt and had an armful of whoopee pies squashed against his chest. He shared them with Ricky and Robby and offered one to Pelé, who nibbled on lettuce instead.

"The twins sure seem friendly with that Somali boy." Grandmère Jeannette appeared from behind and hooked her arm in Jacques's. "I guess youngsters get along easy—easier than grown-ups sometimes."

"Where's Dad?" Jacques asked. "I thought he was coming with you."

"He dropped me off," Grandmère Jeannette replied. "He had somewhere important to go." She quickly looked away and Jacques wondered if she was telling the truth. He also wondered whether the important thing had to do with the Bienvenue Bar at the far end of Main Street.

"Oh, there's Betty Labelle!" Grandmère Jeannette exclaimed. "I wonder if she brought that pretty niece with her. . . ."

Mrs. Labelle came and took Grandmère Jeannette by the hand. "Do you suppose we ought to go over and say hello to the new people?"

"Good idea," Grandmère Jeannette replied. "Let's offer them some of your famous brownies." She turned toward Jacques. "You want to give us a hand?"

Jacques glanced at Kiki and her mother on one side of the room, and then he caught sight of Lucy coming in on the other side of the hall.

"I gotta use the bathroom. . . . Sorry!" Jacques fled into the men's room. As soon as he stepped through the door, though, he wished could turn right back around.

12

Duane was sitting on the edge of the sink, smoking. "Yo! You been avoiding me?"

Jacques inhaled a cloud of gray air and began to choke. "You shouldn't be doing that in here. The alarm will go off!"

"Who cares?" Duane hopped off the sink.

Jacques tried backing away, but Duane came around and stood in front of the door. The dark line beneath his nose had grown in bushy. And his arms were hairy too.

"Listen," Duane said quietly. "This is what's going to happen. Your grandma's shop is two doors down from the Army Navy Store. There's nobody in there at the end of the day except old man Silverstein, and he keeps a lot of cash in the register. I used to work there, so I know. Next Saturday Garth and I are coming by.

"All you need to do is open the back door to your grandma's store. Once we're done at the Army Navy, we'll come in from the alley and go through the bridal shop. When we step out the front onto Main Street, no one will suspect anything. It's easy." Duane stopped and tossed the cigarette butt into the waste can. "You'll get a hundred bucks, I swear."

"I'm not doing it."

"You got no choice, kid." Duane sneered. "Unless you want that pretty Somali girl with the scar to have even more problems."

"What?" Jacques's face flashed hot. "You keep her out of it!"

Duane smoothed the ends of his moustache. "I'm guessing that big brother of hers doesn't know that she's been hanging out with you."

Jacques's bottom lip began to quiver. He bit in deep.

"Thought so." Duane smirked. "You just let us into your grandma's shop for a few minutes, that's all. And you end up with a hundred dollars. Nobody's going to know."

The door swung open. Father Lazar stood in the doorway, sniffing. "You fellows okay in here? "

Duane offered a wide snake smile. "Oh, we're good, Father. I'm helping out my little friend Jacques here." He ducked past the priest.

"I'm okay," Jacques said quickly.

"Why don't you go on back inside now; the party's picking up." Father Lazar held the door open. "And Jacques, you come talk to me if you have any problems, all right?"

Jacques nodded and darted into the social hall. It

took him a minute to realize that something about the party had changed. Instead of Somali families sitting on one side of the room, with church members on the other, the two sides had begun to mix.

Ricky raced by with a fistful of carrots. Jacques blinked; the little boy was wearing Ismail's Ninja Turtles sweatshirt. Robby and Ismail held the treats above Pelé's nose and cheered when the bunny jumped high enough to reach them.

A slim blonde girl was standing behind the twins, holding Baby Amir. When she bent forward to let the baby pet Pelé, Jacques was surprised to see that it was Monique. She looked entirely different. Her hair was combed back, so the red streak didn't show. She wasn't wearing any makeup, and her cheeks were flushed with laughter. Kiki stood next to her, swinging Amir's arms. As Jacques watched, the girls and the baby dissolved into waves of giggles.

Duane was nowhere in sight. He had simply disappeared.

Jacques spotted Lucy leaning against the wall, twirling the ends of her hair as she sipped on a soda. She was wearing skinny jeans and a yellow mohair sweater. Their eyes met and Jacques thought maybe he should go say hey, but he hesitated: what if Lucy got the wrong idea?

Lucy slammed down the soda and marched over to where Kiki and Monique were playing with Baby Amir. She glared at Jacques before settling on the floor next to them.

Gulping hard, Jacques looked the other way. Grand-mère Jeannette and Mrs. Labelle were sitting with three or four Somali ladies, sharing recipes and admiring their colorful dresses. Father Lazar stood nearby, talking with Mr. Silverstein. Jacques noticed that Mr. Silverstein's eyes kept darting to where the women were seated.

Suddenly, Grandmère Jeannette did something really weird. She pulled off her glasses. She can't see a thing without them, Jacques thought. What in the world was going on?

And where was Sammy?

Music started. *Thump-bump, thump, thump-bump.* The beat shook the wooden floor of the social hall. At first it sounded like hip-hop, but Jacques soon realized that the sound was African. The singing was strange and hypnotic.

The music got louder. A few of the Somali boys went to the middle of the room and began to dance. The Somali women stood, swinging their arms and clapping to the rhythm; the other ladies started clapping too. Even Sister Bernadette gently tapped on her knees.

Mohamed came forward and joined the boys in the center of the room. He was even more athletic dancing than he was on the soccer field, twisting and jumping to the beat.

Jacques's eyes bulged. One of the Somali boys was pulling Father Lazar onto the dance floor. The priest shook his head, shrugged, and then with his left hand awkwardly resting on his hip, he began swaying back and forth, bowing out after a couple of minutes with a good-natured sigh.

Finally, Jacques noticed Sammy with Mr. Silverstein and three or four men that he didn't recognize. The men linked arms and began to dance in a circle next to the Somalis. It looked like they were doing the Jewish dance that Jacques had seen at Sammy's cousin's bar mitzvah.

Sammy motioned for Jacques to join them. But before he could decide, the church door opened and Jacques's stomach tightened.

Dad stepped in.

It was plain that Dad had been to the Bienvenue Bar or somewhere like it. His shirt was dirty and unbuttoned, the collar stained with sweat. Dad shifted his feet, holding the doorway for support.

"Where's my boy?" Dad bellowed. "I've come to get my kid, the one who thinks his old man can't hold a job anymore!" Dad staggered forward. He smelled like beer and cigarettes. Grandmère Jeannette jumped up from her chair. "Sweet Mary!" was on her lips. Jacques saw Kiki turn, and one of the Somali women gasped.

Father Lazar and Grandmère Jeannette headed toward Dad, but Jacques got there first. He motioned for his grandmother to stay put, while he grabbed his father's arm. Grandmère Jeannette hung her head, and a sad look appeared in Father Lazar's eyes.

"Come on, I'll help you." Jacques held his breath from the stench as he draped his father's arm over his own shoulder.

After Mom died and they moved in with Grandmère Jeannette, Dad had started staying out late in the evenings. More than a few times, the owner of the Bienvenue, or some other bar, would call around midnight. Jacques and Grandmère Jeannette would have to go fetch Dad and get him up the stairs and into bed.

Jacques tried not to look at any of the faces in the social hall as he turned and led Dad down the steps of the church. The night air pressed cold against his face, but he didn't feel anything besides numb, not even embarrassed. Truth was, he'd gotten used to it. The only thing he hated was the look of pity in people's eyes whenever he had to bring his father home.

13

After the party at St. Francis, things seemed a little different at school. The Somali boy who had played on Jacques's basketball team stopped him in the hallway. He was wearing a Manchester United soccer jersey.

"You are not so bad on the court." The boy had a pointed chin and crooked bottom teeth.

"Thanks," Jacques mumbled. "Sweet shirt, dude."

The boy looked down at his chest. "It comes from my older cousin in England. He sends me his clothes that don't fit. Our family, we are all over the place."

"What's your name?" Jacques asked.

"Yasin."

"I'm Jacques. . . ."

"I know." Yasin grinned and added, "We are in the same math class together."

"Oh yeah," Jacques said, "with crazy Mrs. Woodhouse."

"Yes, she is scary like *Dhegdheer.*" Yasin caught the quizzical look on Jacques's face. "The witch with long ears—all Somali children fear her most!" He laughed easily. "I catch you later, maybe in gym."

"Sure." Jacques wondered if Yasin lived nearby.

As soon as Jacques got to homeroom, he could see that things weren't going to go easy with Lucy. She wasn't talking to him, that much was clear. He tried to say hi, but she twisted around in her seat and began chatting loudly with the girl sitting behind her.

When Kiki sneezed, Lucy walked over and gave her a tissue. Jacques's desk was right next to Kiki's, but Lucy managed to hand out tissues while ignoring him completely.

Sammy caught up with Jacques between classes. "Hey, did you see Boucher carrying Nicole's books?"

"I guess the Sadie Hawkins dance was a big success." Jacques smirked.

"For Nicole, anyway." Sammy grinned back. "So, what happened with Lucy? Did you tell her that you like Kiki?"

"I don't like Kiki!" Jacques replied quickly. "Or Lucy. They're both friends, that's all."

"Oh right." Sammy laughed.

Mohamed strode by. Nothing new there. Mohamed didn't even grunt; his eyes wandered along the ceiling as if he didn't see them.

Boucher passed behind Mohamed's back. "Good luck with practice today, Gagnon!"

"I've got it covered," Jacques replied. But the trouble was, he didn't have it covered at all.

There was no skipping soccer practice. It was his

first day on the field as co-captain with Mohamed. What exactly did Coach Morrin expect? What did the other guys think?

School let out and Jacques stepped into a blast of hot air. Grandmère Jeannette had mentioned something about an early Indian summer, but this was more like steam rising from the sauna at the Y. Was it hot like this all the time in Africa?

When he got to practice, Jacques stretched every limb twice and downed a quart of Gatorade to combat the heat. He felt the team watching him, waiting. Jacques took a deep breath and ran onto the field, but immediately whiffed the ball and missed an easy shot.

"Jackie Jellyfish can't kick straight!" Boucher cupped his hands around his mouth and sang the words.

Jacques kept on trying, but nothing, absolutely nothing, went in.

"Good thing we got until Sunday before our first game," Coach mumbled loudly. He pulled several pieces of gum from his pocket and stuck the wad in his cheek.

Mohamed said little, but there was no need. He dipped and swerved with an easy grace that made Jacques think of him dancing at the church hall. Mohamed made four goals, each one confounding O'Shea, who was a decent goalie.

Even Boucher seemed impressed. "At least we're a lock for the championships." He laughed with a ragged edge in his voice.

After practice, Coach Morrin found Jacques standing in the shade, wiping his dripping forehead.

"You need to take a few more risks out there, buddy."

Jacques cast his eyes on the ground. "I get it."

Coach Morrin sighed and patted him on the shoulder, but that didn't make Jacques feel better at all.

14

Jacques pushed a bowl of cereal back and forth along the dining room table, his stomach slowly churning. He finally shoved the bowl away and walked into the kitchen where Grandmère Jeannette was washing dishes.

"There's something I gotta tell you."

"Okay, shoot." Grandmère Jeannette kept scrubbing.

"The thing is, the first soccer game is Saturday, and I'm co-captain and everything, so I can't come help you at the shop." Jacques cleared his throat and added, "Sorry."

Grandmère Jeannette glanced up, frowning. "That's our busiest day! But I know the first game is a big deal. I suppose I can manage." She wiped her hands on her apron. "How's it going, anyway, with the Somali boy? Mohamed, isn't it?"

"I can't talk; I'm late for school." Jacques's stomach felt sick and better at the same time. He grabbed his backpack to leave.

"One more thing," Grandmère Jeannette called after him. Her voice sounded strangely high. "I might be going out to the speedway on Saturday evening, so you and your father will have to cook for yourselves."

"Oh . . . okay." That was odd. Usually Grandmère Jeannette invited him to go along to the speedway, and usually he said no; he'd rather watch TV or hang out with Sammy. And to be honest, he didn't really want to be seen at the race track anymore with his grandmother. But this time she hadn't even asked.

Jacques hurried home that afternoon after practice. Grandmère Jeannette wouldn't be back from the shop for another half hour, and ever since the church party, Dad had been coming home late nearly every night.

As soon as Jacques reached the apartment, he checked that all the rooms were empty. Then he grabbed the phone and dialed quickly, before he had the chance to chicken out.

A girl answered.

"Is Duane there?" Jacques croaked.

"Wait a minute," the girl replied. "Duane! Du-ane . . . !"

Jacques's heart started beating like it might burst from his chest. "Keep away from my grandmother's shop. I won't do it!" he repeated silently.

The girl got back on the phone. "He's out somewhere."

"Can you take a message?" Jacques asked.

"I guess so," she replied.

"Tell him that Saturday is off. Definitely off! Tell him I won't be there."

"Okay." The girl hung up.

Jacques realized that he'd never even given her his name. Still, his heart was slowing to a dull thump. He felt better, sort of.

The front door squeaked open, and Jacques leapt away from the telephone.

"What's wrong?" Grandmère Jeannette walked in, carrying groceries.

"Aren't you kinda early?" Jacques exclaimed.

"Young people shouldn't be so jumpy." She set the bags on the table. "It was slow toward the end of the day, so I closed up and stopped at the Save-and-Shop."

Grandmère Jeannette placed two cartons of milk in the refrigerator. "By the way, I ran into your Coach Morrin while I was shopping. He says he don't really need you on Saturday."

"What do you mean?" Jacques was suddenly short of breath.

"The game is on Sunday. You must of heard him wrong. You'll have to miss some of practice, but he says he can spare you." Grandmère Jeannette folded the bags and stuck them under the counter. "You better come by the shop at one, and I'll have you lock up at five."

"But Grandmère . . ." Jacques began.

"But nothing," Grandmère Jeannette cut him off. "You've done it before; it's easy. I'd ask your father, but the truth is, the way he's been acting these days," she lowered her eyes for a moment, "I trust you more— though don't you ever tell him that!" She blinked and nodded. "It's all settled."

Jacques clenched his jaw. It didn't seem fair that he always had to worry about Dad. Still, Jacques didn't say a word. He knew it wasn't his grandmother's fault that after Mom died, his father had never been able to pick himself up and move on.

15

The rest of the week was a jumble. Mohamed dominated every practice, scoring effortless goals from impossible angles, while Jacques barely held his own. Jacques prayed he might come down with something catchy by the weekend, but on Saturday morning he woke up feeling perfectly well. He could always say he had a stomachache and get by with Dad, but he knew that he could never fool Grandmère Jeannette.

Jacques cut out of practice early and dragged his feet along the sidewalk on his way to the bridal shop. He paused at every cross road and nearly jumped out of his skin when he saw a skinny kid in a hooded jacket standing in front of the library. As soon as the kid turned, though, Jacques snorted with relief; it was just a weirdly tall girl from sixth grade.

When Jacques passed by the Army Navy Store, Mr. Silverstein waved to him through the display windows. Jacques waved back but wondered why Mr. Silverstein was wearing a bow tie to spend the day selling cargo pants and hoodies.

By the time he reached the bridal shop, Jacques felt better. The sun was shining through lazy clouds. It was just an ordinary Saturday. Duane was all talk, and always had been. How a kid like that could ever get a girl like Monique to marry him was impossible to figure.

Jacques went to check that the alley-side door was locked, then settled into tidying the showroom and hanging up gowns. He only twitched a little when the front bell jingled.

Grandmère Jeannette smiled broadly as she stepped forward to greet Mrs. Labelle, who walked in with Lucy right behind her.

"*Bonjour* Jeannette, *comment ça va?*" Mrs. Labelle offered enthusiastic air kisses. "My niece is going to a wedding next month, and she needs a pretty dress. I told my sister you could find us a nice bargain." Mrs. Labelle whispered the word *bargain* while Lucy rolled her eyes. "It's gonna be first class. They're having a band up from Boston."

Jacques looked at Lucy, who immediately turned the other way and stamped one foot.

"*C'est bon!*" Grandmère Jeannette exclaimed. "Of course we'll find somethin' real special." She glanced sideways at Jacques as she took Lucy to the sales rack. "I have just the perfect dress for you, *chérie.*"

"I'm going to get a Coke," Jacques blurted out. "My throat hurts wicked bad."

Jacques fled through the door and onto Main Street.

Yvonne's House of Pizza was a block and a half away, next door to the library. Jacques hadn't had any lunch and couldn't remember whether he'd eaten breakfast. He plunked down at the cracked Formica counter in front of the restaurant window and ordered two slices. Across the street, a group of Somali kids were coming out of the library. When he spotted Kiki on the steps, Jacques jumped from the stool and hurried outside.

"Hey," Jacques called over. "What are you doing here?"

"Oh hi! The library has free tutors today." Kiki smiled. "But to tell the truth, they are not as good as you at explaining math."

"You want something to eat?" Jacques pointed to the pizza place.

Kiki licked her lips as she shook her head. Two Somali girls stood in the doorway behind her, staring.

"What about later?" Jacques asked.

"Mohamed has a job with Mr. Silverstein, and I am supposed to meet him at the mosque when he is done." She nodded toward a simple storefront on the side street behind them.

"Your brother is working at the Army Navy Store?"

"Only for today," Kiki replied. "Mr. Silverstein asked him at the church party. He will help move some heavy things. Hooyo has not found work yet, so the pay is good for us." Kiki motioned toward the Somali girls, who were beginning to giggle between whispers. "The tutor will start again soon. I should go back."

Jacques shuddered as he turned away. Mohamed

at the Army Navy Store? What if . . . ? He bent over his knees and sucked air. It was a good thing, maybe. There was no way Duane would try anything now. No way at all.

When he walked back into the bridal shop, Jacques was whistling.

"You feelin' better?" Grandmère Jeannette stood at the cash register counting bills.

"I'm sorry. I, um, forgot to eat lunch."

"Hmmm . . ." Grandmère Jeannette lowered her glasses. "I was wondering if Betty Labelle's pretty niece was the reason you were so shy about coming here today?"

Jacques shrugged.

"You haven't made that girl any promises you can't keep, have you?"

"Grandmère!" Jacques exclaimed. "Lucy is just a friend!"

"Aha, I see. . . ." Grandmère Jeannette's lips curled slightly as she closed the register.

Three or four ladies came in to browse, but there were no more sales. Still, Grandmère Jeannette smiled and hummed as she dusted the counters and fitted plastic covers over the gowns. At exactly four o'clock, she disappeared into the ladies room. When she returned, she was wearing a different blouse and dangling earrings.

"I'm going to the bank now. All you need to do is lock the doors at five, and you can go on home." Grandmère Jeannette picked up her purse. "Make sure your father eats somethin' for dinner, okay?"

Jacques nodded. Then his pulse began to race. "Grandmère . . ."

"Yes?" She paused by the door.

Jacques gulped. "Be careful at the speedway, that's all. Lots of creeps hang out there."

Grandmère Jeannette smiled and blew him a kiss. Her cheeks were rosy, and her lips looked especially pink.

The door closed, and the shop went quiet. Jacques glanced through the windows up and down Main Street, but there was nothing to see. He sighed and wondered whether he could close up early. With a yawn, Jacques turned and squatted next to the pile of half-made boxes on the couch.

The front door jingled, and Monique walked in.

"Oh—it's you." Blushing, Jacques sprang to his feet.

Monique's hair was pulled back to one side in rows of tiny braids. Her nails were black and shiny. "I figured I'd come find something I like." She touched the small silver cross around her neck.

"Yeah, sure." Jacques motioned toward the rack of wedding gowns.

"Maybe more like this one." Monique pointed to a mannequin wearing a short red cocktail dress. The mannequin's golden hair was twisted in elaborate curls, and her skin was the color of chalk.

"Can I ask you something?" Jacques glanced at Monique.

"I seem kind of young to be getting married, is that it?" Monique didn't look up as she ran her nails over the silky fabric.

"No, of course not! It's just that you're really—I mean, you're pretty and you're smart and everything. . . ."

Monique didn't answer, but her eyes opened wide when Jacques said the word *smart*.

The phone started ringing in the upstairs office.

"I'll be right back." Jacques bounded up the stairs wondering if Grandmère Jeannette was calling to remind him about something important. He also wondered whether Monique thought he was the stupidest kid in middle school.

There was crackling on the line, and then a strange nasal tone. "This is Maine Premier Bank calling. I must inform you of a serious delinquency on your mortgage."

Jacques covered the phone with his hand, which was starting to tremble. Before he could think what to say, he heard a sharp rap from the back of the shop.

Monique's voice cut the air: "Duane! What are you doing here?"

16

Jacques dropped the phone and raced down the steps, but it was too late. Monique had already opened the alley door.

Duane stood inside the doorway grinning, a wild look in his eyes. His hair was slick with sweat, and his arms were wrapped around a camouflage backpack.

Garth stood behind him panting and cradling one fist. Jacques could see that his knuckles were bruised red and purple.

"Anyone else in here?" Duane's grin hardened into a sneer as he pushed Jacques aside.

Jacques shook his head. "You need to go! You have to leave *right now*."

"We'll be gone soon enough." Duane motioned for Jacques and Monique to stay quiet. After checking that the dressing room was empty, he crept into the show-room and crouched by the front door.

Jacques tried to follow Duane, but Garth's good hand landed squarely on his shoulder. Jacques and

Monique stood back with Garth, a few feet behind Duane. They could see through the display windows to the street.

"What's going on?" Monique glanced sideways at Jacques's flushed face.

There was some kind of commotion outside. A policeman ran by with his radio flashing, and people were gathering in a circle on the sidewalk.

Duane reached up and cracked the front door open. Suddenly, a muffled scream rose from the crowd: "Call an ambulance! He's hurt bad!"

Jacques could barely breathe; his heart was pounding *think! think! think!* Maybe he could bust out and yell for the police, but Garth's fingers were deep in his shoulder, pressing to the bone. If only he had closed the shop early, turned Monique away . . . or warned poor Mr. Silverstein that Duane was planning something terrible.

"Do you hear an ambulance?" Monique whispered. The sirens were faint at first, but getting louder.

Duane took a stained envelope from the backpack and tossed it on the couch. "We're outta here." He grabbed Monique by the wrist.

Garth smacked the side of Jacques's head before slipping out the door. "You keep your trap shut, understand?"

"Leave him alone!" Monique exclaimed as Duane pulled her into the road. Her face was pale and her blue eyes were fluttering, scared. They disappeared down Main Street, away from the crowd.

As soon as they were gone, Jacques stuffed the envelope in his jeans and ran outside.

A man was lying on the sidewalk, blood pooling beneath his head.

Jacques cut through the huddle and fell to his knees beside Mr. Silverstein. His head was matted and swollen, but at least Jacques could see that he was breathing.

Mr. Silverstein's eyes opened slowly, watery and bloodshot. "Jacques . . . would you tell Jeannette that I'm sorry?" he whispered.

"It's gonna be okay!" But Jacques had no idea how badly Mr. Silverstein was hurt and whether it would ever be all right.

The ambulance arrived, and the paramedics jumped out. "Stand back! Give us room."

As Jacques rose, he noticed Mohamed in front of the Army Navy Store, shaking his head wildly. Two police officers were with him. A block away, from the direction of the library, Kiki was coming toward them. She was walking fast, her long skirt swinging. Then she broke into a dead run.

Jacques felt someone behind him. He turned and swallowed hard when he saw Grandmère Jeannette's stricken face.

"You go ahead home now. Lock the shop and go home."

"I don't know what happened," Jacques began. "I heard the sirens and . . ."

"I've got to get to the hospital. You go back home to your father." Grandmère Jeannette hurried to where the paramedics were preparing to load Mr. Silverstein into the ambulance. She bent forward and smoothed his lips with her fingertips.

So there it was. Grandmère Jeannette and Mr. Silverstein.

Jacques's hands were shaking as he locked the door of the bridal shop. A police van pulled up, and he watched as Kiki and Mohamed climbed in.

Jacques jammed the key in his pocket and ran as fast as he could toward home.

17

"Dad! Dad . . . ! Quick!" Jacques burst into the apartment yelling.

Dad sat at the dining room table, holding a can of beer. A pile of bills lay scattered in front of him. "What is it? What's wrong?"

"Mr. Silverstein was robbed and hurt bad! Grandmère Jeannette went with him to the hospital. We gotta go right away." Jacques's limbs were shaking.

"Sit down." Dad motioned to the table. "Take a seat and tell it to me straight."

Jacques gasped for air, but stayed on his feet. "We have to help! The police might have arrested Mohamed."

"Whoa—what? Who are you talking about?" Dad's eyes narrowed. "Do you mean the Somali kid from the soccer team?"

"Yes . . . Mohamed was working for Mr. Silverstein today. Someone broke into the Army Navy Store, and Mohamed didn't have anything to do with it, but

Mr. Silverstein got hit in the head, and now he's in the hospital." Jacques's eyes were beginning to swell.

"Slow down a minute." Dad grabbed Jacques by the arm and pulled him into the chair. He wiped his lips with the back of one hand. "Listen buddy, I'd go over to the hospital right now if I could. But I don't suppose I'm in any shape for driving."

Jacques glanced behind his father to the wastebasket in the corner. It was full of empties.

"There's no reason to be worrying. Your grandmother can always get a cab home." Dad paused and took a long swig of beer.

"What about Mohamed?" Jacques demanded, but didn't wait for an answer. He ran into his room and buried his face on the bed.

"Come on back here!" Dad hollered, but Jacques ignored him.

Jacques pounded the pillow with his fists, then pulled the dirty envelope from his pocket and peered inside: there were five crumpled twenty-dollar bills. He felt the tears come in waves, over and over, until he fell into a fitful sleep.

In the middle of the night, Jacques thought he heard the front door open. Turning onto his back, he listened, but the air was silent; maybe it was only a dream. Jacques squeezed his eyes shut and tried to think of soccer combinations, his favorite players— anything, *anything* besides the terrible thing he'd let happen.

And then he prayed. A short, raspy whisper that

drifted softly above his head to the ceiling: "Please God—it was all my fault. I should have warned Mr. Silverstein! Please don't let him die."

When Jacques woke, he was lying on top of the bed, still wearing his clothes from the day before. The shades were high, and sunlight streamed through the windows. For a split second, he thought about the first soccer match, and whether he could pull out from his slump. But when Jacques lifted his eyelids, the dirty envelope was still there, laying on the pillow next to him.

An ocean of nausea rolled over him. He stuffed the envelope under the bed, took a deep breath and went into the living room.

Grandmère Jeannette was settled in a lounge chair, fast asleep. The dining table had been cleared and the wastebasket emptied.

Jacques touched her arm gently.

"What? Oh *cher*!" Grandmère Jeannette blinked and sat upright.

"Mr. Silverstein, is he . . . ?" Jacques lost the words. Every limb was shaking.

"He's going to be okay." Grandmère Jeannette rose and gave Jacques a quick hug. "He has a concussion, but thank God, the wound wasn't deep."

"Do the cops know who did it?" Jacques dug his fingernails into his palms.

She shook her head. "Someone hit him from behind. He didn't see anything."

"The policemen took Mohamed in their van!" Jacques exclaimed.

Grandmère Jeannette sighed. "Louis—Mr. Silverstein—has a heart of gold, God bless him. He was kind to that Somali boy and was trying to help him."

"But Mohamed didn't have anything to do with it!" Jacques pounded one fist into the other.

Grandmère Jeannette looked into Jacques's eyes. "You have a good heart too, *mon cher*—but what do you know about this boy? You've already told me that he stays to himself, and that he gets real angry sometimes."

"He didn't do this! He couldn't have! He was just working there today because he needed money for his family."

"How bad did he need the money, I wonder?"

"No!" Jacques shouted. "It isn't like that!" He saw the surprise on his grandmother's face and lowered his voice. "We've *got* to help him."

"I'm going back to see Louis after church this morning." Grandmère Jeannette stretched and rubbed her cheeks. "Maybe he'll remember something more. In the meantime—you keep your distance from Mohamed. I don't need two of my fellows in the hospital." She smiled weakly. "There, my secret is out."

"Mohamed is innocent," Jacques whispered as Grandmère Jeannette headed to her room.

Jacques wiped his eyes and went over to the picture of Mom on the dining room hutch. Looking at her picture made his stomach hurt even more. After slowly tracing her lips with his fingertips, he placed the photograph face down in the bottom of the drawer and closed it tight.

18

Pelé's hind foot was thumping hard against the rabbit hutch. Jacques lifted him from the cage and rocked him in his lap as he sat on the bed, trying to think. Did the policemen take Mohamed and Kiki to the station? Had they been there all night? In a cell?

It was all his fault. He should have stopped Duane! How could he make it right? Would Mr. Silverstein ever believe that Mohamed was innocent?

Grandmère Jeannette poked her head into Jacques's bedroom. "Time for church. I'm going to the early Mass so I can get straight over to the hospital."

"I . . . can't go now," Jacques stammered. "I have to get ready for my soccer match." He coughed loudly. "I'll try to go later, I promise."

Grandmère Jeannette sighed. "That's right, your first game's today. I wish I could be there to watch you shine, *mon cher.*"

"It's okay," Jacques replied quickly. "You tell Mr.

Silverstein that I . . . that we're pulling for him." His tongue felt like gum stuck in his throat. "Grandmère . . ."

She leaned on the door frame, waiting.

"It's just that . . . the truth is," Jacques lowered his voice and looked down at Pelé, "I'm not really good at being co-captain. Mohamed's better than me, way better."

Grandmère Jeannette bent forward and stroked Pelé's nose. "Nobody's perfect! You go ahead and lead those boys the best you know how. That's plenty enough." She gently lifted Jacques's chin and smoothed a curl from his forehead, then blew a kiss as she left.

There was still no sign of Dad. Jacques put Pelé back in his cage and stuck a Post-it on the fridge—Home Soon—without even knowing where he was headed. He rushed down the steps and jumped on his bike.

To the left, the police station; to the right, the hospital. Jacques glanced back and forth twice. Then, he began to pedal like mad.

He quickly reached the old apartment building where Kiki's family lived. Laundry hung over the porch railings, and Ismail's Ninja Turtles sweatshirt was flapping on a line. Jacques biked past the front of the building, around the block, then back again. A face appeared in the doorway, and he pulled on the brakes. In half a minute, Kiki came flying out.

"What are you doing here?" she asked, breathless. "Is Mr. Silverstein all right?"

"He's gonna be fine," Jacques answered. "He has a

concussion, but Grandmère says it's not as bad as it looked."

Kiki rubbed her cheeks and sighed. "Mohamed was so worried! He has been up all night. Me too."

"What happened with the police?"

"They asked many questions, then they took us home."

Jacques exhaled.

"But they want Mohamed to come back to the police station with Hooyo tomorrow after school."

Jacques's fingers felt cold and slippery. "Did your brother see who did it?"

"No! Mohamed was down in the basement the whole time, moving boxes. He heard something and ran upstairs, but it was too late." Kiki's eyes grew wide. "Hooyo is very scared. She says if Mohamed gets into trouble, we could all—they could make us go away."

Kiki stopped and lightly traced the scar with her thumb. "My father told us we would have a safe life in America. It was his dream for our family to be safe."

"*I promise you,*" Jacques said softly, "it's going to be okay."

"You are positive?" Kiki's bottom lip was quivering.

"Yes." Jacques coughed and looked away. How could he promise her that? If he told on Duane, the police would surely come for him. He could get arrested, and since Duane had escaped through the bridal shop, maybe Grandmère Jeannette would get into trouble too.

"We've got the first soccer match today; I better get moving." Jacques gripped the handlebars.

"Good luck with the game." Kiki wiped her eyes with the edge of her hijab and went back to the house.

Something was moving in one of the upstairs windows. As Jacques pushed off, he thought he saw the outline of Mohamed's face, flickering in the glass.

19

Jacques rode his bike out toward the lake. The houses drifted away as he pounded on the pedals, trying hard to focus. He circled the lake and stopped by the small rocky beach to throw stones in the rippling water before heading back to town.

By the time Jacques reached the soccer field, the sky had gone dark. Pine trees and the spires of St. Francis stood out against black-bellied clouds. There was a distant crack of thunder, and as if on cue, Sunday church bells began to ring.

As Jacques approached the field he could tell immediately that something was wrong. A huddle of boys with grim faces stood kicking at the ground with their cleats, while Mohamed sat alone a few feet away, hugging his knees. Jacques searched for Sammy, but it didn't look like he'd arrived yet. He'd have to do this alone.

He jogged up just in time to hear Boucher cursing.

"We're not playing with that kid! It was bad enough Coach made him co-captain, but my uncle says he's a thief. If old man Silverstein dies, Mohamed could go to jail for *murder.*"

O'Shea turned toward Jacques. "Hey Gagnon, I heard you were there when Mr. Silverstein got robbed."

"Did you see Mohamed whack him?" Boucher made a slamming motion across his body.

"Shut up, you jerk! It *wasn't* him." Jacques spit the words in Boucher's face. "You're nothing but a stupid A-hole!" He said it all without thinking, but the weird thing was, for the first time in two days, Jacques felt his shoulders relax.

Boucher's eyes went blank before sinking into black darts in his head. He pulled one arm back for a punch, but Coach Morrin got there just in time to grab it.

"We got a game to play!" Coach Morrin barked. He turned to Jacques. "Get the boys on out there! It's time to start."

Jacques took a deep breath and stood straight. He dribbled the ball away from the huddle and over to Mohamed. "Let's go!"

Mohamed sprang to his feet and nodded once.

The other team was from Purgatory Hills. Everybody knew their guys were tough. Someone said the captain's brother had been kicked out of school for breaking a kid's arm, and Jacques believed it.

As they ran onto the field, Jacques saw Sammy's car round the corner. Sammy jumped out while it was practically still moving and flew on the field. O'Shea and the other boys glanced toward Boucher and hesitated for a moment. Then, slowly at first, they followed after Jacques.

He let out a long sigh. The boys weren't coming fast, but at least they were coming. Boucher hung back, but with Coach Morrin pointing the way, he finally jogged to midfield, put his hands on his hips and spat.

At the very top of the bleachers, a yellow umbrella twirled against the gray sky. Lucy was sitting behind it. She lowered the umbrella and offered half a wave, so nobody else could see. Jacques relaxed his fist and wagged two fingers in her direction. He was glad she was there, he suddenly realized, really glad.

The whistle blew and the ball was in play. Purgatory scored a quick goal before Boucher got possession and weaved his way down the field. It looked like he might make it, but a huge defender overtook him. Boucher kicked the ball to Sammy, and Sammy sent it to Jacques. With a fake to the left, Jacques got the ball to Mohamed, who broke through the pack. The Purgatory boys raced forward but couldn't catch him. Mohamed chipped the ball over the goalie's head in a perfect arc.

As he jogged past, Jacques instinctively reached out, and Mohamed lifted his hand to knock knuckles. Man, his hands were strong.

At the beginning of the fourth quarter, Lakemont was holding its own but still losing by one point. They needed a goal to tie. Jacques got the ball and flicked it ahead of him, dodging and dancing, sprinting down the field. As he neared the goal, he felt a surge of excitement.

Suddenly, two enormous boys were behind him and closing in fast. To his far right, Mohamed picked up speed and broke ahead of the pack. In a split second, Jacques crossed the ball to Mohamed's left foot. Mohamed jerked his leg up, and with a tremendous crack, volleyed to score. Jacques watched the ball slip past the heads of three defenders and into the goal just before he noticed a baboon-faced boy sliding in from the side. He felt his legs knocked away as he flew into the air. Jacques landed with a dead thud, his jaw hitting the ground first. It took a minute to breathe. Crap.

When Jacques opened his eyes, Mohamed was towering over him, hollering at the kid from Purgatory and pulling on his shirt. "What you doing? You bull crap do that move one more time, and I come after you!"

Jacques rolled up. At first his jaw was numb, then a searing pain beginning at his ear streaked down the side of his face. A red card was floating in the air above him.

Coach Morrin appeared, yelling at the ref, "What the hell are you doing? My kid didn't even touch him!" His voice became a roar. "We got a guy hurt on the ground! You're carding the *wrong boy!*"

"Take that one out, now." The ref glared at Mohamed. "Or this game is over!"

Mohamed snorted, shifting from one foot to the other, his Adam's apple bobbing. Coach took Mohamed by the elbow. "Come on."

Mohamed hesitated, then ran over to Jacques. He bent down, resting his hand on Jacques's shoulder. "Get to it, man!" Mohamed turned and jogged off the field alone.

Jacques pulled himself up. His chin felt tender and was starting to swell, but nothing seemed broken.

Coach Morrin loomed above him, puffed with purple rage. "You okay to play?"

Jacques's face felt like it was being squeezed between two rocks, but he grunted, "Yeah, I'm good."

"Annihilate those guys." Coach flicked his fingers toward the baboon-faced boy from Purgatory, who was grinning like he'd eaten a tiger.

Jacques waved his arms as Purgatory kicked the ball into play. The players tore off, racing down the field.

Get to it.

Jacques forgot about everything in the world except the soccer ball. He pushed his cleats deep into the grass and ran, smashing the ball from side to side, down the field and into the goal. Score! Jacques quickly got possession and scored again—two quick goals before the buzzer rang out.

Behind him Jacques heard cheering. Boucher and O'Shea were tearing off their shirts and jumping on each other's backs while Sammy and the other guys whooped and hollered. Up in the bleachers, the yellow umbrella was spinning like a top.

The ref yelled for them to get off the field. The game was over.

"Way to go!" Coach Morrin pumped both fists in the

air. He motioned for the boys to line up and slap hands with Purgatory. The second he was through the line, Jacques ran for his bike.

A single shard of lightening split the clouds as Jacques began to pedal. He could see the spires of St. Francis ahead. In the distance, Mohamed was walking away from the field, his shoulders hunched as the storm moved in.

Get to it.

Rain fell on Jacques's nose and dripped into his eyes as he bumped along the potted road. He dropped his bike on the slick lawn in front of St. Francis and rapped on the door. No answer. He caught his breath and knocked again, harder, louder.

Father Lazar cracked the door open, one arm raised against the rain. "Oh, Jacques—your grandmother was here this morning, but she's already left for the hospital." Father Lazar squinted as he took in Jacques's swollen face. Jacques wasn't sure if his cheeks were soaked with rain or tears, but it was too late to check.

"There's something I need to talk to you about, Father. Something bad."

"You're getting wet, son," Father Lazar replied softly. "Come on in." He swung the church door wide and pulled Jacques inside.

20

"Mr. Gagnon, are you with us?" The clock behind Mrs. Sinclair's desk was ticking so loudly that Jacques didn't hear his name being called for Monday morning attendance. Mrs. Sinclair walked over and stared down at him. "Is anything wrong?"

He sat up and shook his head, no. When would Kiki come? He wanted to tell her the truth. He wanted to say that he would go to the police station after school and explain what happened. That even if he got in trouble, he'd do it. He'd make sure that Kiki's family wouldn't have to worry. Even if he got kicked out of soccer, even if he got suspended from school, he would tell what happened and set things right.

Even if Kiki never talked to him again.

But where was she? The clock kept ticking, but Kiki never showed up for homeroom. As soon as the bell rang, Jacques hurried out to search the hallways. He wasn't sure exactly what he would say to Kiki, only that he had to say it.

The hall outside the classroom was empty, but when Jacques turned the corner in front of the lockers, there was Kiki, squatting on the floor. Her head hung over her knees, and she was dabbing her eyes with tissues.

Jacques ran to her side. "What happened?"

"The police came this morning." Kiki choked. "They took Mohamed! Hooyo went with him to the station."

"No! No way!"

"Hooyo sent the little ones to the neighbors and told me to come to school, but I did not want Mrs. Sinclair to see me like this. I don't know what to do." Kiki covered her mouth with both hands. "What if the police think Mohamed robbed the store? What if they believe he hurt . . ." She couldn't finish.

A group of Somali girls came rushing toward them. Jacques felt like he might be sick, right there in the hallway.

"I'm going to fix this! Just hang on, okay?" Jacques's heart was racing. He wrapped his arms around his chest and sprinted to the front of the school.

A security guard, heavy and slow, stood by the entrance. Jacques veered and ran down the opposite corridor. Sammy was leaning against the wall in front of the gym.

"Hey dude . . ." Sammy stopped. "What's the matter?"

"I gotta get out of here, quick! But there's a guard standing in front."

"Try the door in the basement—it goes out by the woods." Sammy pointed to a narrow flight of stairs.

"Thanks! I'll tell you everything later." Jacques

bolted through a small utility door at the bottom of the steps and dashed across the school yard, through the bushes and into the trees.

When he finally slowed down, Jacques noticed that his legs were scratched and bruised. At least nobody was coming after him. Jacques took off again, running as fast as he could all the way to the Lakemont Police Station.

21

Jacques rushed up the granite steps to the station. "MOHAMED DIDN'T DO IT!" pulsed inside his head. As he pulled the heavy doors open, he nearly ran into an elderly lady leaning on a cane. Jacques jumped sideways, apologizing. But before he could enter the station, a policeman blocked the doorway.

"Aren't you Donny Gagnon's kid?" The policeman eyeballed Jacques. "I played football against your pop when we were in high school. He had a great arm." The officer cocked his head, exposing the tattoo on the back of his neck. "What are you doing here?"

"I . . ." Jacques gasped. "I need to talk to somebody! It's about the robbery on Main Street."

"Oh yeah?" the policeman stopped smiling. "What's the problem?"

"It's just that . . . I might have seen something," Jacques stuttered.

"What'd you say?" The officer's walkie-talkie was

buzzing. He put one finger to his lips and moved aside to answer.

Jacques waited on the step, staring at his sneakers and trembling. He heard the door swing open again and did a double take; Monique walked out.

She stopped short and grabbed his arm. "You don't need to be here."

"What do you mean?"

"I spoke to the police already. I told them everything."

Jacques held his breath. "Are you sure?"

"Duane and Garth confessed. They pled guilty right away so they could get a lighter sentence." Monique leaned close to Jacques's ear. "And believe me, after what Duane did, I won't be needing that wedding gown anymore. You were right. I *am* too young to be getting married."

"What will you do instead?" Jacques asked. With her face that close, Monique looked just like a kid.

"Community college." Her eyes lit up. "I might even study fashion design." Jacques felt the tips of Monique's fingernails graze his cheek. "You be good, okay?" She bounced down the steps without looking back.

"What were you just saying about the robbery?" The officer put the walkie-talkie back in his belt and tapped Jacques on the shoulder.

"Um, well . . ." Jacques covered his mouth and coughed hard. "I was really . . . you know, my dad was worried about Mr. Silverstein. He's a friend of my grand-mother's. Kind of a good friend, actually. She's alone a lot in her store."

"Oh, that's right," the policeman said. "Your grannie has the bridal shop a couple doors down from the Army Navy, correct?"

Jacques nodded quickly.

"Listen, you don't need to be concerned about your grandmother's safety. We caught the punks responsible." The policeman snorted. "Believe me, there won't be any more robberies."

"Thanks, officer. My grandmother will be glad." Jacques turned and started down the steps.

"One more thing," the policeman called after him.

Jacques froze.

"You tell your pop that I'll see him at the next reunion game, okay?"

Jacques flashed thumbs-up. He walked a few feet away and looked over his shoulder to make sure the policeman had gone back into the station. Then he dropped his head below his knees and drank air. He felt relieved . . . though not exactly better.

A minute later the doors opened, and Mohamed came out with his mother behind him. Mohamed raised his hand when he caught sight of Jacques. He left his mother standing by the bottom of the steps and jogged over.

"Hey," Jacques said.

"What you did at the game, in front of the other kids . . ."

"It was nothing." Jacques shook his head. "Boucher's been a jerk since preschool. He had it coming."

"Boucher is not so smart, but he kicks the ball hard." Mohamed's lips curled into a crooked grin.

Jacques cleared his throat. "There's something else." His voice squeaked as he forced the words out. "Your sister and me are friends. Just friends—that's all."

"I talked to her." Mohamed nodded. "I know you been okay with her. You showing her respect."

Jacques took a deep breath. "So . . . we good?"

"Yeah. We sure good." Mohamed reached forward to high five. "I have to go home with Hooyo. I see you at practice."

Jacques glanced at the woman waiting by the steps. She was wearing a long black hijab, and in daylight she didn't look as much like Kiki as she had at the church party. Her forehead was lined, and there were dark circles beneath her eyes. But when she looked up at Mohamed, her face shone with the same bright smile.

22

"Your school called. They said you skipped class yesterday. What's that about?" Grandmère Jeannette peered at Jacques over the top of her glasses while she poured a second cup of coffee.

"That's weird," Jacques replied. "I swear I was there." Jacques crossed his fingers under the dining room table. "I better finish breakfast so I won't be late."

Grandmère Jeannette grunted with an I-dunno-what-you're-up-to look and took a long sip from her mug. "Well, there's somethin' else. Louis wants to see you."

"What?" Jacques spit out two Cheerios.

"Mr. Silverstein asked that you come to the hospital."

"But I'm a kid; they won't let me in there."

"First off, you're nearly a teenager now." Grandmère Jeannette added more cereal to the bowl. "And anyway, they let everybody visit. You go on over there this afternoon. Tell him I'll swing by at the end of the day after I close the shop."

Jacques opened his mouth, but nothing came out.

"Finish eating and scoot. I don't want to hear about any more missed school. Understood?" Grandmère Jeannette pushed her glasses up the bridge of her nose and began clearing the table.

Jacques dropped the bowl in the sink and went to his bedroom to get his backpack. Why did Mr. Silverstein want to talk to him? Had he seen something? Did he know about the money? He shivered and dropped to the floor. Pulling the envelope from under the bed, Jacques counted five crumpled bills. He stuffed the envelope in his pocket; it felt heavy as stone.

At school Kiki was pacing in front of the blackboard. Her tongue darted back and forth between the gap in her teeth. Mrs. Sinclair made everyone quiet down early.

"We have Communication Time for homeroom this morning, and I've asked one of your classmates to present something special. She's a tiny bit shy, so please give Kiki your full attention." Mrs. Sinclair put one finger to her lips and stepped out of the way.

Kiki came to the front of the room. She was holding a piece of yellow lined paper. "My family came here from my country, Somalia. It's in the east of Africa. There was a terrible war, and we heard that America was a good place, so we came to get away from the fighting." Kiki glanced down at the paper. "This is a poem that I wrote. With Somali people, poems are a big thing for us." She cleared her throat, and Jacques noticed that the paper was shaking slightly.

> *"My people are strong,*
> *My brothers are strong,*
> *I am strong.*
> *We make our path, we struggle,*
> *To live together in peace."*

Kiki paused for a minute and lowered the sheet. She gazed above the desks and toward the ceiling as she continued by heart in a loud, steady voice.

> *"My father is gone now,*
> *His bones are mixed with sand.*
> *I see him in my dreams.*
> *Oh country, oh father!*
> *Do not cry for us.*
> *In this new place, our new country,*
> *We do not forget,*
> *We keep your strength,*
> *We are your strength; you protect us all."*

Kiki stopped and exhaled. The room was silent.

"That was wonderful—thank you." Mrs. Sinclair's voice cracked a little.

A boy on the opposite side of the room put his hand in the air. "What did your father do? I mean, what was he?"

"He was a doctor," Kiki replied.

Lucy spoke up. "Do you want to be a doctor too?"

Kiki cocked her head, thinking. "Yes, I do. Or maybe even a writer."

The bell rang, and everyone gathered their stuff to go. Jacques followed Kiki into the hall. "I didn't know you could write poems like that."

"You got your math, and I got my words." She grinned.

Jacques waited until all the other kids had passed. He hesitated, scratching the back of his neck. "I've been wondering about your dad. . . . I mean, did he die in the war?"

Kiki paused, twisting the end of her hijab. She looked up and down the empty hallway, took a long slow breath and nodded. "Three soldiers came to our house in an old truck. I was in the yard playing with our goat when I saw them. I did not know why they were there, but I could tell they were angry, so angry. Two of them had rifles, and one held a long knife." Kiki closed her eyes. Her fingers reached to the top of the scar and slid to her lips. "The goat ran away, and the soldier lifted the knife. He was stabbing something, and then I . . . I couldn't see. I heard my father come running out from the house to stop them. But the soldiers took my father instead. They carried him into the truck, and he was gone."

Jacques felt like his own chest had been torn apart. "That's horrible."

"It's okay." Kiki's eyes opened wide. "It happened a long time ago."

"Sometimes, I wish I was as brave as you," Jacques whispered.

Kiki shook her head and smiled. "I think you are already."

23

By the time Jacques made it to the hospital, it was nearly four o'clock. Maybe Grandmère Jeannette had been wrong. . . . Maybe kids weren't actually allowed to visit. Or maybe visiting hours were already over, and they'd turn him away. But the lady behind the reception desk pointed to the elevator, and when he got off at the fourth floor, a nurse brought him down the hallway to a bare white room with two beds.

Mr. Silverstein was sitting in the second bed, reading a newspaper. Jacques passed by the other patient, asleep and snoring softly. The top of Mr. Silverstein's head was bandaged, and his forehead was several shades of blue.

"Hello Jacques! I'm glad you came, very glad." Mr. Silverstein gestured toward the small chair beside him.

Jacques sat down, one hand deep in his pocket, fingering the envelope with the hundred dollars inside. "Why did . . . I mean, Grandmère said you needed to see me?"

Mr. Silverstein dropped the newspaper onto the

nightstand. "I'm going to get straight to the point, okay? You and I both know there is something we have to talk about."

Jacques's head felt light, and the walls of the room turned fuzzy. "I . . . I'm sorry—really sorry!" he blurted out. "I never wanted any of this to happen."

Mr. Silverstein leaned forward. "Listen, I know things are difficult, and I see how much your grandmother depends on you. But I've been doing a lot of thinking, and this whole incident has made me realize something."

Jacques flinched, eyes cast down, prepared for Mr. Silverstein's anger. What would the punishment be?

"I've known your grandmother for a good many years now—you too."

Jacques glanced up. What was Mr. Silverstein talking about?

"To be perfectly honest, Jacques, it's been lonely since my wife died, very lonely. My daughter lives far away, in New York. Seeing your grandmother smile is about the only thing I look forward to these days." Mr. Silverstein hesitated and maybe even blushed. "I guess I've said too much. But man to man, I want you to know that I care about your grandmother, and that I hope you and I will be friends—good friends."

Jacques squirmed. "Was that . . . that's why you wanted to see me?"

"Yes." Mr. Silverstein chuckled softly. "I guess that's all."

The door was there, so close by. The other man was

118

snoring. Jacques could walk out and down the corridor, right there and then, and Mr. Silverstein would never know, nobody would ever know what he'd done. He could throw away the envelope so there'd be no fingerprints, and even if Duane said something, Duane was a thief, and he was going to prison—nobody would ever believe him.

Jacques's breath came in short jerky waves as he glanced at the open doorway. Slowly, he pulled the envelope out from his pocket and placed it on the bed in front of Mr. Silverstein.

"I'm sorry. I tried to stop Duane, but he wouldn't listen to me." Jacques shrugged. "But I *didn't* stop him, so I guess it's all my fault."

Mr. Silverstein lifted the envelope; a twenty-dollar bill peeked out. He was quiet for a minute, his brow in knots, staring at the money. "You'd better tell me the whole story, son."

Jacques began as far back as far back as he could remember, when he was just a kid at church with Mom. He told Mr. Silverstein how Duane would steal his weekly charity money, and how he was afraid to say anything because Duane's aunt was Mom's friend. And later, how Duane tried to get him to sell pot at school.

Finally, Jacques told Mr. Silverstein about Duane's plan to rob the Army Navy Store—that Duane had threatened him, but had also thrown a hundred dollars on the couch for him to keep.

"Mohamed had nothing to do with it." Jacques's head hung low. "Please believe at least that much."

"I only wish you had said something." Mr. Silverstein's furry eyebrows arched below the bandages. "Before all this happened, I mean."

Jacques pressed his palms into his forehead. His face was burning, and his eyes stung. He didn't care anymore what the punishment would be; he deserved whatever he got.

"It happened to me too, once," Mr. Silverstein said softly.

"What?" Jacques raised his head.

"When I was about your age, there was this kid on our street who shoved me down and took my lunch money. Nearly every day, for months this went on! It wasn't so much the bruises, but the humiliation that hurt so terribly."

"Was he a really big dude?" Jacques asked.

"It was a girl, not a dude." Mr. Silverstein rubbed his temples, remembering. "And no, she wasn't actually that enormous. Her name was Margie. She was a year older than me, and I was scared stiff of her. I didn't dare tell anyone. I was afraid everyone would laugh."

"But . . . how did you make it stop?"

"Eventually, I grew tall, and Margie didn't dare push me around like that." Mr. Silverstein wiped his lips. "But it was really no joke at the time."

He picked up the envelope. "I want you to do something for me. I want you to take this money and bring it over to St. Francis. I understand that Father Lazar is collecting funds for the new African families—helping them buy furniture and such."

Jacques nodded quickly. "Okay."

"And one more thing. . . ." Mr. Silverstein held out the bills. "You need to tell your father what you just told me."

"But . . . I can't!" Jacques exclaimed. "He . . . he won't understand."

"No 'buts,' Jacques," Mr. Silverstein replied. "You've got to talk this over with your family. . . . Agreed?"

Jacques bit deep into his lip. Dad would be furious to think his kid wasn't strong enough to fend off a loser like Duane. But Mr. Silverstein's eyes were dark and steady. "Yeah . . . I promise."

The frown on Mr. Silverstein's face relaxed, replaced by a lopsided grin. "You like to fish, Jacques?"

"Fish?" Jacques had no idea what to say.

"I love to sit by the lake. It's very peaceful," Mr. Silverstein continued. "Perhaps we'll all go together one day soon. Jeannette says she's handy with a fishing pole, but the way she holds onto the end like it's a fry pan, well . . . I just don't know if I entirely believe her." He chuckled. "I've got a lot to learn about your grandmother!"

On the way home from the hospital, Jacques stopped by St. Francis. He stood straddling his bike for a few minutes, staring at the stained-glass windows and stone facade. A seagull landed on the roof and began to caw. What was a gull doing so far from the ocean? Jacques was startled when Father Lazar appeared beside him.

"It's a magnificent church, isn't it?" Father Lazar

gazed up to the top of the spires. "Our grandparents and great-grandparents came from Quebec without much education, didn't speak the language and worked in the mills for next to nothing. But they pulled together and created this beautiful place. They made a home here."

Father Lazar checked his watch. "I'm off to visit an elderly parishioner. I'll see you at Mass this weekend."

After Father Lazar left, Jacques walked around to the social hall entrance. Imbedded in the wall was an old marble plaque that he'd hardly noticed: "St. Francis Building Fund." He was surprised by how many of the family names he recognized. And then, the most familiar popped out: *"Jacques and Jeannette Gagnon."*

Jacques thought about the photo in Grandmère Jeannette's wedding album, the one of his grandmother in her fancy lace gown with her handsome young husband beside her. His grandfather had dropped out of high school and worked double shifts in the mill in order to save enough money to buy the bridal shop. He had died two years before Jacques was born.

Under the plaque, there was a wooden barrel with a slit at the top and a sign that read: "New Mainers Fund." Jacques drew the five crumpled bills from his pocket and stuffed the money in.

He suddenly imagined Grandmère Jeannette with a fishing rod. That was something he couldn't wait to see!

24

Jacques got on his bike and slowly headed home. He knew he had to keep his promise to Mr. Silverstein, but when he tried to imagine telling Dad the truth, he pictured his father blazing with fury.

As he rode past the library, Jacques caught sight of Kiki on the sidewalk with Nicole. The two girls were so busy chatting that Nicole didn't even look up. She was showing off a new purple jacket that matched the fringe on her purse. Kiki waved and Jacques nodded, but kept on pedaling.

Jacques's head was throbbing as he rounded the last corner. As the house came into view, he slammed on the brakes and skidded to the curb. Dad was sitting outside on the steps.

"Hey there, I've been waiting for you."

Jacques jumped off the bike and let it clatter to the ground. "Is something wrong? Is Grandmère all right?"

"Nothing's the matter. I just wanted to talk."

The grass, the house, the sky—everything was whirling. Had Mr. Silverstein already phoned? Did Dad know exactly what he'd done?

Dad opened his mouth, but before he could speak, Jacques sprang to the steps and touched Dad's knee.

"There's something I have to say." In one long breath, he explained how Duane had bullied him and tried to make him help rob the Army Navy Store.

Dad's cheeks began to puff in and out. His neck popped in tight chords, and his right fist jutted forward, punching air. "Are you telling me Duane asked you to steal from Louis Silverstein?"

Jacques winced like he'd been socked in the stomach. He was sorrier than he'd ever been in his whole life.

"I know it was wrong." Jacques slumped against the steps waiting for Dad to yell how weak and stupid he'd been—and how lucky it was that Mr. Silverstein was alive and that Jacques hadn't ended up in jail.

But instead, Dad glanced down and rubbed the corner of his eyes. "Did he hurt you?"

"No." Jacques was stunned to see that Dad's eyelids were damp. "It wasn't like that. Duane just wanted money."

"I always knew that kid was trouble!" Dad slammed the back of his heel against the stair so hard that it sounded as if he'd cracked the wood. "Why didn't you say anything?"

"I guess I thought I could handle it . . . that I could make Duane stop," Jacques slowly answered.

"This should have never happened. I should've been

there to help. I got drunk and let everyone down." Dad's mouth was wavering, and his voice turned to gravel. "Sometimes, I miss your mother so much I don't know what to do. You were just a little guy when she . . . when the accident happened. Do you remember her? I mean, the small things?"

And then, there she was, so close in Jacques's head, smiling and holding something furry. "Mom liked kittens."

"Yeah." Dad snorted. "She loved all critters. Always bringing them home! Cats, dogs, strays. Remember the half-beagle, half-shepherd she found wandering in the yard? That hound was one ugly mutt, but she didn't care; she loved it. Maybe that's kinda like the same thing she saw in me." Dad looked straight at Jacques. "Most of all, she loved you. Anything you needed, anything you wanted, she'd just make it happen."

Jacques suddenly remembered the night before Halloween when he was six or seven. He had his heart set on a Spider-Man costume, but it cost too much. Mom came home and found him crying. She dried his tears and went straight to the sewing machine. When Jacques woke up in the morning, there was a shiny red and blue outfit on the end of his bed.

Mom could always make things right. If only she was still alive. . . . If only.

"You're the one thing in my life that matters." Dad's hand rested heavy on Jacques's shoulder. "After your mother died, you were the reason I got up every morning."

Jacques tried to say something, but his throat was too tight.

"I'm getting help. I started one of them programs to stop drinking. I got a sponsor—somebody to make sure I don't start hittin' the bottle and screw up again."

Jacques swallowed hard. "That sounds good."

Dad wiped his face with a sleeve, then reached behind his back and pulled out a square brown box. "Whoa, I almost forgot. This is for you."

"What is it?"

"Late birthday present, I guess. Go ahead. Open it."

Jacques pulled off the lid. A shiver, the good kind, went down his spine. It was a regulation Arsenal jersey. And it looked brand-new.

"Isn't this too expensive?" Jacques smoothed the shirt against his chest.

"I got a break from my pal at the sports shop." Dad cocked his head, nodding. "And anyways, it turns out we've got something to celebrate for a change."

Jacques sat up straight. "Really?"

"Louis Silverstein's asked me to manage the Army Navy Store."

"Honest? For always?"

"Just 'til he's on his feet. . . . But after Christmas, my old boss says he'll take me back so long as I'm sober." Dad paused. "And I swear to you, I swear on my life that I will be. We're gonna be okay. We'll make it."

Dad reached out his hands, and Jacques took them. Big hands, football hands, squeezed tight.

"It looks like I'll be seeing your Somali friend—he'll be helping out at the Army Navy on weekends."

"Mohamed got a job there too?" Jacques exclaimed.

"Yup. Your grandmere's beau seems like a real solid guy."

"Apparently, Mr. Silverstein wants to take her fishing." Jacques grinned.

"Fishing?" Dad looked sideways. "But . . ."

"Grandmère hates fish, I know!"

They both began to laugh. Then Jacques laughed so hard that he snorted twice and his stomach hurt, and he couldn't stop to catch his breath.

"Listen, so long as we're talking like this—any girl caught your eye yet? I noticed Betty Labelle's niece circling around you at church. She's plenty cute."

Lucy and her yellow umbrella flashed through Jacques' mind. "I better go do my homework." He stretched and started up the stairs with the soccer jersey tucked under one arm.

"Okay, but believe you me, someday soon, a girl is gonna get your attention."

Jacques paused, thinking about the "J" on Lucy's binder.

"And when she's got a real pretty smile like your mom, it's the best thing that can ever happen." Dad flashed thumbs-up with a faraway look in his eyes.

25

TWO WEEKS LATER

Grandmère Jeannette paraded through the apartment with a long feather duster, vigorously brushing each piece of furniture. She even dusted the top of Pelé's cage. It seemed awfully early on a Saturday morning to be so busy.

"Sweet as pie to take a day off . . ." she muttered to herself as she dusted all the windows. Grandmère Jeannette had arranged for Betty Labelle to watch the shop so they could have a family day at the lake with Mr. Silverstein, now that he was out of the hospital and on the mend.

Dad and Jacques sat on the couch with steaming mugs and the sports section of the *Lakemont News*. When Grandmère Jeannette stepped in front of them, Dad nearly spilled his coffee.

"Wicked nice hat you're wearing!" Dad exclaimed.

"But where in blazes are you going dressed like that?"

Grandmère Jeannette shoved two gray locks under an orange cap with metal studs and casting flies stuck to the back. She was wearing a green and yellow plaid flannel shirt, sleeves rolled high. The shirt and hat didn't exactly match.

"As a matter of fact, the hat was a present from Louis. He says it's the best thing for . . ."

"Fishing?" Dad slapped his knee as he began to chuckle.

"What's so hilarious?" Grandmère Jeannette frowned. "Louis says it looks good. Just right."

"Well, he would say so!" Dad wiped drips of coffee from his jeans.

Jacques covered his mouth with one hand, but he knew his grandmother could see him laughing.

Grandmère Jeannette dusted the top of Dad's head and marched toward her bedroom. "You boys need to be at the lake by three o'clock. And don't be late. Louis is the punctual sort."

Dad winked at Jacques. "Looks like she means business. You and me better stay on best behavior."

After soccer practice, Jacques helped Dad pack the Honda with coolers and the barbeque grill. Grandmère Jeannette said that she'd meet them at the lakefront park with Mr. Silverstein.

They drove past the old mill and the apartment building where Kiki and Mohamed's family lived. A couple of doors down, in front of a large building with chipped stucco and peeling trim, Jacques spotted Yasin in the yard. He rolled down the window and yelled, "Hey!" as they went by.

"You know somebody who lives there?" Dad asked. "Is that one of the Somali boys?"

"Yeah," Jacques said. "We play basketball together sometimes."

"Do you recognize the place?"

"No. Should I?"

"That's where your mother and I lived when you were born. We had a tiny apartment on the fifth floor; your room was practically a closet. It was hardly much, but we were happy." Dad shook his head. "I won't ever forget the day we brought you home—all those stairs with us carrying one of them baby car seats. And you squawking the whole time!"

Jacques turned and took another look as they passed by. He wondered if Yasin might be sleeping in the very same room.

Orange and copper leaves covered the pebble beach at the lake. It was getting late in the season; the park wasn't crowded. A couple of older men and a few young Somali boys were fishing from a wooden dock.

The back of the pond was ringed with evergreens, and the water sparkled along the rocks in the autumn light. Mr. Silverstein was right, Jacques thought. It was pretty and peaceful. Usually he just didn't notice.

Jacques helped Dad set up the barbeque and

unpack the coolers. Suddenly, Dad elbowed him and pointed. He could see a couple at the far edge of the beach, near the woods. Mr. Silverstein was casting a line in the water while Grandmère Jeannette watched. His arm swung above his head and whipped forward with surprising grace. Mr. Silverstein was wearing red suspenders over a black checkered shirt, and Grandmère Jeannette had on her orange cap. From a distance, Jacques thought, they both looked a lot younger. Suddenly, Mr. Silverstein slipped one arm around Grandmère Jeannette's waist and guided her hands along the fishing rod. Wait . . . was Grandmère Jeannette *giggling*?

"Let's leave the love birds for the time being, shall we?" Dad pulled out two Cokes and threw hot dogs on the grill. "By the way, I'll need your help with chores tomorrow."

"There's a girls' soccer game in the morning," Jacques said quickly. "I'm kind of supposed to be there."

"Ladies soccer, huh?" Dad grinned. "Somebody special on the field?"

"Coach Morrin wants the guys to show support, that's all."

Dad flipped the hotdogs and nodded. "Coach is right. We can do the work in the afternoon."

When Jacques looked up, Grandmère Jeannette and Mr. Silverstein were walking toward them. Grandmère Jeannette had the fishing rod in one hand and was holding something gray and shiny with a white belly in the other. Her hair fell in loose curls below the cap, and her lips were open in the broadest grin Jacques had ever seen. Hanging from a hook in Grandmère Jeannette's left hand was a long fat bass for dinner.

26

The next morning Jacques pulled on his new Arsenal jersey and headed over to meet Sammy and Tim O'Shea on the way to the girls' match. By the time the boys got to the field, a group of kids had already gathered on the sidelines.

Lucy held a large neon poster with GIRL POWER written in capital letters and underlined twice. She was wearing a chunky green cardigan that made her eyes glow. When Lucy spotted Jacques she raised the sign higher and screamed, "GO, GO, GO!" even though the players were still warming up. She paused and glanced over her shoulder. "Hey."

"Hey," Jacques mouthed back. His heart was racing, but it was good, all good. Maybe he and Lucy could go get pizza after the game.

Mohamed and Yasin walked up beside them.

"We going to see what the girls can do!" Mohamed exclaimed.

Jacques grinned at the guys and nodded. "I heard some of them aren't half bad."

Suddenly, Lucy whistled and waved her sign furiously toward the field. "Jacques, isn't that . . ."

A tall man wearing a COACH jersey was sprinting in front of the team.

"What the heck?" Sammy exclaimed. "It's your—"

"Dad!" Jacques shouted.

Dad turned and jogged toward the boys as Jacques ran onto the turf.

"What are you doing here?" Jacques gasped.

"See that man over there, the girls' coach? He's my sponsor, the one that's helping me with the drinking. So now I'm the assistant coach. His idea of therapy, I guess."

"Why didn't you tell me?" Jacques's mouth was still open.

"Thought I might surprise you." Dad stretched his arms and grinned. "Can't say I know that much about this game, though. You up for showin' your old man a few drills later on?"

"Sure, yeah. We could practice at the park."

The ref blew the whistle to begin. Dad saluted and ran back. The boys watched as Lucy and Nicole led the crowd in a synchronized wave.

"Hey, look over there!" O'Shea pointed to the far end of the field. Jacques turned just in time to see the ball spinning through the air. A girl wearing a blue head scarf and long baggy gym pants was coming down from a header.

Jacques pivoted, grabbing Mohamed's arm. "What's going on? Is that Kiki? She didn't tell me! I thought . . ."

"Coach Morrin explained to Hooyo that girls who play soccer can get college scholarships. So Hooyo spoke to all the family, and she decided to let Kiki try." Mohamed ran his tongue over his lips. "Coach says boys can get the scholarships too."

Somebody booted a corner kick to the top of the penalty box, and Kiki lunged forward. In an instant, the ball hit the inside of her foot and flew into the air. The other girls slowed down to watch the ball speed toward the far edge of the goal, while the goalie tripped and rolled in a futile attempt to stop it.

"She scored!" Jacques grabbed Sammy's shirt. "Kiki got one in!"

The rest of the team surrounded Kiki in a group hug.

"Not too bad." Mohamed knocked knuckles with all the guys, while Lucy and Nicole danced in circles.

Jacques watched as Kiki flew across the field. She was every bit as fast as her brother, dodging left and right and making contact with the ball with the same natural ease.

"GO, KIKI! GO!" Jacques yelled as loud as he possibly could.

Kiki turned for a split second and raised both arms in the air. With a quick twist, she swung to the left and raced away, chasing the ball like nothing could ever stop her.

ACKNOWLEDGEMENTS

Writing is a labor of love, and many whom I love help me write. THANK YOU to my many friends and colleagues at Westport Writers' Workshop, including Maggie Mudd, Valerie Leff, and Susan Lynton, as well as friends and readers Laura Toffler-Corrie, Sari Bodi, Christine Pakkala, and Michaela McColl, who listened over the years and poured over my prose—smiled when something was good and shook their heads when something was dreadful.

Special thanks to my writing mentors: Suzanne Hoover, for her unfailing sense of craft and razor sharp nuggets of wisdom, and Pat Reilly Giff, for simply being the kindest, most generous, and encouraging role model in writing and in life.

It was Pat who first raved about my amazing editor, Mary Cash. Thank you, Mary, for bringing out the best writing with sensitivity and care. And grateful thanks to my terrific agent, Susan Cohen at Writers House, for believing in this book, and her ace assistant, Nora Long, for her helpful comments.

My childhood home in Maine, which in recent years experienced a large influx of Somali immigration, was the inspiration for this story, and my father, who sought out any and all opportunities for cultural exchange when I was a child, is a secret character here, along with my remarkable mother, who came to America as a refugee and was the wedding gown saleswoman extraordinaire at our family bridal shop.

I could not have done this book without the help of wonderful, inspiring Somali teen readers. It was a privilege to see the experience of growing up in Maine through their eyes. Thank you for sharing your lives and for showing me how strong and resilient kids can be.

Big hugs to my children—yes, especially you, Sarah—not only for reading, but for answering every last question I ever have about what a kid in *any* particular situation just might think.

To my brilliant and darling husband, thank you for smiling through it all, or most of it. It was when you liked it, that I finally thought it was good.

And lastly, heartfelt thanks to Mrs. McDonald, my fourth grade teacher at Lake Street Elementary School, who let me stay inside at recess and write.